MARRIAGE LOST AND FOUND

BY

TRISH WYLIE

MILLS & BOON®

For Owen
Who fought hard to stay in this world
Your courage and determination are inspiring

First published in Great Britain 2005
Large Print edition 2005
Harlequin Mills & Boon Limited,
Eton House, 18-24 Paradise Road,
Richmond, Surrey TW9 1SR

© Trish Wylie 2005

ISBN 0 263 18602 4

Set in Times Roman 16½ on 18½ pt.
16-1105-47432

Printed and bound in Great Britain
by Antony Rowe Ltd, Chippenham, Wiltshire

PROLOGUE

It was in the gap between Christmas and New Year's, when people started thinking about what the New Year had to hold. About brighter and better things to come. About New Year's resolutions to help everything along in the right direction. That was when she made the decision to let go.

Now, as to the year they were leaving? Well, Abbey Jackman had had a pretty good year. A pretty *darned* good year, in fact. Her career prospects were good. She was doing a job she loved surrounded by talented, smart people. She had moved into her new apartment less than a month ago and even had a new, highly motivated 'boyfriend' since October. Even her emotionally dependent mother had managed to find a new beau to distract her from constantly poking into her daughter's life. Oh, yeah, life was good.

Abbey had spent several years dealing meticulously with her outward appearance, her social circle, those little details that should lead her towards the life she wanted for herself. And now it was paying off.

She'd done the 'reality check' thing, the 'leave behind all the things that had held her back' thing, and the 'escaped to bigger and better things' thing. Everything was finally going according to plan. Abbey was in charge of her own destiny for the first time in a long, long time.

There was just the one tiny detail left undone.

With her feet curled beneath her on the sofa, she chewed on the end of her pen and stared into the middle distance. The letter was just so hard to write. Even now. Realistically she didn't even know if it would get to him because she didn't actually know where he was. Where had his life taken him? It still bugged the hell out of her that she even cared about those things.

She shook her head. All she could do was send it on to his last base with his service number on it and hope that some wee soul would forward it on. Because eight years was long enough...

Hell, two, three and four years should have been long enough! But back then, even after the time had passed her by, a part of her had still held a glimmer of hope. For the romance of it all, the meant-to-be. The things she'd believed in once upon a time. Reality had killed those dreams off along with her unfounded hope, and now it was time to move on. To let go.

Romance just wasn't the way she had thought it should be. She now knew it had to be more about building a solid foundation. About practicality, stability and reliability. All those things were realistic, and more long-lasting than the wild, seat-of-her-pants love affair her memory had held onto for so long.

They had both been young then. Still idealistic. It made sense that something so magical could never have lasted into 'real life', right? Real life didn't consist of magic. Except in very small and short-lasting instances.

She knew all this stuff now.

But even after eight years the letter was still hard to write. Crumpled balls of cream writing paper all over her living room floor bore testimony to that fact.

At least if his name had been John she could have started the letter with the traditional 'Dear'…

She tried out everything from 'Hi there' to plain old 'Hello' to the more formal 'Dear Mr Wyatt'. But nothing seemed to fit. 'Dearest Ethan' still held a tad too much of that long-ago emotion. So she was pretty much stymied from the first damn line!

With a sigh she threw yet another crumpled ball of paper onto the ground in front of her. Why was this still so *hard*?

It wasn't as if he'd made any attempt to come find her. He'd known her address, known where she lived. In fact her mother still inhabited the same big old house they'd had for most of her life. So it wasn't as if he couldn't have written a letter. Made *some* attempt. But he hadn't and that still hurt.

Abbey felt her heart cramp in her chest. *Damn him.*

Pushing her writing pad to one side, she stood and paced the floor in oversized fluffy socks. *She'd* lived up to her part of their great magical plan. She'd come home to wait, to finish her education as they'd agreed and to prepare herself for their new life together. They'd really been very sensible about the whole thing considering how fast it had happened…

But then he'd disappeared, abandoned her and the dreams they'd talked about for their future. *Together.*

And then her father had died and the world had been an empty, lonely place.

No, she could never forgive Ethan for breaking the promises they'd made. For taking away the magic. She couldn't go back and make it all right again.

Abbey was just going to have to get on with the business of letting go. Pure and simple. It was time. She squared her shoulders, took a breath and closed her eyes for a second. Finding her strength sometimes just took a moment. Especially when it came to letting go of Ethan.

Wasn't it always that way with a girl's first love?

Marching resolutely to the sofa, she grabbed her pen and pad. After all, she was an adult now. In charge of her own destiny. Enough was enough.

Her pen moved across the paper in fluid strokes. Suddenly words came, and she was letting the dream go.

CHAPTER ONE

'HAPPY birthday, Abbey.'

It was approximately the twenty-fifth time she'd heard the words, but it was nice when they came from people who knew her so well. It made turning thirty not quite so bad.

It made turning thirty and having the party in the tiny town she'd once called home seem bearable. *Just.*

'My, my, sweetness, has the entire population of this tiny place turned out for you?' Karyn Jamieson, her closest friend from the city, leaned towards her. 'Is there anyone who *isn't* related to everyone else here?'

Abbey smiled. 'Not really. Welcome to small-town life.'

'This place doesn't qualify as a town. A town has more than one main street, and there's a place name at either end of that street, not just the *one* end.'

Karyn had driven up in the dark from Dublin and in the previous evening's dim light had driven right through the town before she'd even realized she was in it. That happened a lot when people visited Killyduff. In truth, the people of Killyduff quite liked it that way.

Outsiders were treated like escaped convicts, eyed with suspicion and questioned at every available moment. The Gestapo would have had nothing on the deadpan inquisitors of the inhabitants of Killyduff. Abbey knew that only too well. Karyn and a handful of other courageous souls made up a meagre group of friends from Dublin who had been brave enough to make the trip to be with her.

But still, a part of Abbey—a very small, carefully controlled part—would have missed not having her celebrations 'at home'. Not that she was likely to confess that fact to her mother in the current millennium. After all, she'd done a lot of her growing up here. It couldn't do any harm, on a momentous occasion such as a thirtieth birthday, to take a step back and remember where she'd come from.

That didn't of course mean that she wasn't highly optimistic about her fortieth birthday being celebrated somewhere entirely more interesting.

She reached out and patted her friend's forearm. 'One more day, pet, and then you can head back to civilization.'

'Mmm.' Karyn looked sceptical. 'But at the first hint of me wearing anything vaguely tweed in origin I want you to shoot me.'

Abbey laughed. The thought of Karyn in tweed was quite something. If it didn't come straight off the pages of a fashion magazine she wasn't interested. 'I promise.'

'Happy birthday, Abbey.'

Abbey smiled her best 'birthday smile' as she was hugged and kissed on the cheek by the local postman. She swapped pleasantries about how much she'd grown up and how the good life was treating her in the city. Then she turned back to her friend. 'Promise me something in return?'

'Name it, birthday girl.'

She leaned closer. 'Promise me that next year we'll celebrate in Antigua.'

Karyn's eyes sparkled. 'From your mouth to God's ears, sweetie.' She nudged her hard. 'But maybe you should speak to the lovely Paul about that one.'

Abbey's dark eyes swept across the room to Paul. He was every mother's dream for her daughter, and at that moment Abbey's mother was predictably glued to his side. Elizabeth Jackman adored him, in an almost hero-worshipping manner. Probably relieved her argumentative daughter had actually managed to find a man at all. But somehow, in his designer suit with his magazine-cover good looks, he seemed out of place in the tiny country hotel where all great Killyduff parties were held.

She smiled as he nodded across at her. He was just such a great guy. She kept telling herself that. A great guy, ideal for the new life she'd made for herself. Handsome, wealthy, successful, patient. Husband material.

The smile disappeared from her face when he looked away. So why did it feel as if there was still something missing?

She took a sip of her drink. 'If Paul had his way it would be a honeymoon.'

Karyn gasped. 'He proposed?'

'I guess it's the next logical move, isn't it?'

'Have you accepted?'

'I'm thinking about it.'

Her friend's perceptive green eyes studied Abbey's face intently for several moments. 'So why aren't you grinning like an idiot and making a big announcement about now? This would be the perfect place. Your mother would be thrilled.'

Abbey thought for a moment, considered hiding behind the shadow of a small untruth and then decided to unburden instead. 'I just don't know that I want to be married—' She hid her face in her glass to stop anything further from escaping her lips.

'You try really hard to hide behind this career-girl image, don't you?'

It crossed Abbey's mind that there were a great many larger things she hid.

'No. I believe in marriage, in partnership, in the whole spending a lifetime with one person. I really do.'

'You're just not sure that someone is Paul.'

'I should be.' Her eyes flicked across the room to him again. 'He's perfect.'

'Obviously not.' Karyn's eyes followed the same path. 'Or you would have said yes by now.'

'Maybe. Maybe I'm just not ready yet. What can I say?' She smiled ruefully at her friend again. 'I'm screwed up.'

'Hell, aren't we all?' They looked around the room for a few minutes before two more locals sidled up to say the obligatory, 'Happy birthday, Abbey.' Then Karyn pursed her lips before asking, 'So what's missing?'

Seat-of-the-pants passion, that moment of heart-stopping recognition that it was the real thing?

That same experience she'd had once before.

She knew the answers that jumped unbidden into her mind were heartfelt. It irritated her beyond words that she hadn't managed to retrain herself better in that department. She'd known what she wanted in a husband all too clearly back in the day.

She thought again about the letter she'd sent after so much inner debate. Would it have killed him to answer her? To set her free? To allow her to say 'yes' unconditionally to Paul, the great guy who was so suited to her new life?

'I don't know.'

'You should have a fling. The down-and-dirty kind.'

Abbey's eyebrows rose at the statement. 'You think? And how would that help exactly?'

Karyn shrugged elegantly. 'It would make you see if what you have with Paul is real. I'm telling you, some wee empty fling would soon put you back on track again. Like that guy I was telling you about earlier. The one I saw checking into the hotel.'

Abbey knew who she meant. Karyn had gone on about him at heated length through dinner. Apparently he was a 'bit of all right'. Abbey knew that that meant he was brief-fling material in Karyn's eyes and very little else. Abbey, however, didn't have the time or the inclination for that. It wasn't in her long-term plan.

'You should have invited him along. At least if you were drooling over him, you'd be distracted from small-town life.' And from Abbey's lack of commitment to an ideal man.

They both knew how easily distracted Karyn was by a hot male.

'I did.'

'Well, when he arrives you can bring him to meet Paul.' Her eyes sparkled. 'We can do a comparison and if he looks like the kind of guy I should fall all over I'll just drop Paul like a hot potato.'

Karyn noted the sarcasm in her words. She was perceptive that way. 'Oh, I'll bet you will. We all adore you for that impulsive nature of yours.'

They both smiled as Abbey began to move them in Paul's general direction. She leaned her head towards Karyn as they walked. 'What can I say? When you have a plan the best way to make it work is to stick to it.'

Paul's blue eyes sparkled at her over her mother's head as she approached. Without a word he stepped to one side and allowed her to fill the space beside him.

'Hey, gorgeous.'

'Hey.' She planted a kiss on his smoothly shaven cheek and smiled as she wiped the slight smear of lipstick she'd left behind. 'Missing me?'

'Abigail, you've only been away from him for ten minutes.' Her mother edged closer to his other side. 'He's hardly had time to miss you.'

And why would he when he had her vivacious mother for company? Being a teenager under the shadow of her gorgeous mother had been difficult at times, but now that she was older she had more confidence in herself. In theory.

Paul snaked his arm around Abbey's waist and drew her to his side. 'How could I not have, Liz? She's as captivating company as her mother.'

Abbey smiled up at him. He always said the right thing at the right time. It was what made him such a terrific negotiator in business.

'I just hope Abigail doesn't let you get away, Paul. That kind of devotion is rare in young men these days.'

'And not in Alan, Mother?' She couldn't help herself. Abbey's mother's choice in a new beau still rankled. The man was ten years younger than her and way too smooth for Abbey's personal taste, but the simple fact was he wasn't her dad. And she still missed her dad. Every day.

Elizabeth bristled at her daughter's question, a spark in her pale eyes. 'Darling, I think you already know I think Alan is perfect. And if any part of his character was imperfect, he has me to smooth it over, doesn't he?'

Of course he did. Lucky guy. Abbey actually felt a small pang of sympathy for him. Her mother knew exactly how to get what she wanted out of people. The gift of manipulation.

But then who was Abbey to criticize when it came to relationships? She already carried enough of a past to sink the *Titanic...*

The tall man watched the small group from across the crowded room. He felt...*empty*, when he'd expected to feel—what exactly? A sudden burst of emotion towards the woman he'd once been so involved with?

Maybe it had been too much to expect, after all. He hadn't realized how much he'd persuaded himself it would all make sense when he saw her.

But to have flown thousands of miles to this tiny Irish town to expect one person to piece the puzzle of the last eight years together was a stretch, wasn't it?

His hazel eyes blinked as he watched her interact with those around her. Watched as she moved closer to the fair-haired man's side, smiled up at him. His stomach twisted. He didn't like that scene much. But then if he'd been in her shoes, waiting around for someone to turn up for years, wouldn't he have moved on too? Ethan discovered that even though it made sense in his mind, it apparently didn't mean he'd like it much.

Interesting. *Curious*, but interesting.

'Oh, my Lord. He's here.' Karyn gasped as she glanced past Abbey's shoulder. 'Don't look round!'

Abbey raised an eyebrow. 'If I don't look round, how can I see him?'

'You don't have to see him, you can take my word for it.'

'Who's here?'

Abbey glanced at Paul. 'Some hot guy that Karyn chatted up earlier.'

Paul took a deep breath. 'Oh, one of *those*.'

Karyn frowned at him. 'Yes, I know it's difficult for you to hold back your raging jealousy in public, sweetie.'

'I've managed for years, haven't I?'

'Beautifully.' She tilted her head and smiled sarcastically before looking back over Abbey's shoulder. 'He really is gorgeous, though, don't you think?'

Abbey tried to turn again.

'No, don't look!'

'Oh, for goodness' sake. How can I give an opinion when I can't see through the back of my head?'

Elizabeth turned. 'The dark-haired man by the bar? I don't think I know him.'

And that was saying something. Elizabeth Jackman knew everybody in Killyduff within a few hours of them arriving. She was practically head of the gossip committee.

'Oh, hell, he's coming this way.'

Abbey smiled at her friend's palpable excitement. When was the last time she herself had had a reaction like that?

She watched Karyn's eyes as they gradually moved up to look at the man, felt the air displace slightly behind her and was about to turn when a deep voice sounded.

'Hello, A.J.'

Her breath caught in her chest and she slowly turned to look up into familiar hazel eyes. It couldn't be. Couldn't be, but it was. He was here.

'Ethan.'

Ethan smiled a slow, lazy smile at her. 'Happy birthday.'

Karyn moved slightly to stand at their side. 'You know this guy?'

Abbey's heart pounded noisily against her ribcage, her eyes still refusing to believe what they saw in front of her. She'd thought about it for so long. What she'd say and do, every reaction rehearsed a million times over in waking and sleeping moments. And when it came down to it, she'd managed his name. Stunning repartee.

'You could say that,' she murmured.

They continued staring at each other as Paul and Elizabeth moved closer too.

'I don't believe we've met. I'm Abigail's mother.'

Ethan turned slightly and smiled more broadly. 'It's nice to meet you.'

'You're American.' Paul stated the obvious.

'Yes, I am. And *you* are?'

'I'm Abbey's boyfriend.'

Ethan raised a dark eyebrow as Paul shook his hand. 'That's nice.' He glanced at Abbey from the corner of his eye, still shaking Paul's hand as he added, 'I'm Ethan Wyatt. Abbey's husband.'

'You're *married*?'

Abbey glared angrily at Ethan as her mother's voice took on a shrill tone. 'How can you possibly be married? This is a joke.'

'No.' Ethan allowed Paul to pull his hand away. 'No joke. We've been married eight years, apparently.'

The damned cat was out of its bag. That was the thing with secrets. Eventually they jumped out to bite you on the—

But this wasn't exactly the place she wanted everyone to find out about it, was it? Here in the tiny rumour mill of her home town, surrounded by everyone she'd kept her secret from. And on her damned birthday too! His timing sucked beyond belief. How dared he? How bloody dared he?

She frowned hard at him, her voice icy. 'We're *divorced*.' She spoke the words she knew had to be true by now.

'Actually—' he looked her straight in the eye '—we're not.'

'What do you *mean* we're not?' Abbey had always assumed he'd have done something to fix things by now. He obviously hadn't thought too much of the vows they'd made. And surely it would have been easy for him to have hopped to somewhere like Mexico or wherever it was they went in the movies for a quickie divorce.

'Did you file for a divorce here?'

'No.'

'Well, I didn't where I come from. It takes two to make a divorce. So that means we're still married.'

Her eyes widened. 'What do you mean you didn't? How the hell have you let this go on all this time and not done anything about it?'

'I could ask you the same thing.' His face remained calm. 'In fact, there's a lot I want to ask you.'

And that wasn't a one-way street. She glanced away from his face to Paul's. Poor Paul, who was staring at her with a frown. 'You're really married to this man?'

She nodded slowly. 'I should have told you.'

A flush of sheer embarrassment crawled up over her cheekbones. She'd always thought she *would* tell him some day, that he'd maybe even laugh at her *naïveté*. But a part of her just hadn't been able to. It was too close to the bone, it had still smarted that she could have been so very stupid. Paul respected and admired her and she hadn't wanted to lose that.

'Yes, you should.' His voice grew sharper. 'Some time before I proposed would have been nice.'

Ethan turned his head. 'You proposed to her?'

'That's none of your damn business.'

'I think you'll find it is. A husband should know these things.'

Paul took a step closer to him, his chest growing broader. 'If you're her husband then where exactly have you been all this time?'

Good question. Abbey stepped between them, her back to Ethan. 'This is a long story and here isn't the place to talk about it.'

Paul reached for her arm and tugged her forwards. 'Then we'll talk about it outside—'

Ethan immediately grabbed hold of her other arm, halting her escape. 'I think you need to let me talk to my wife first.'

'She's not your wife.' Elizabeth stepped into the fray. 'Let go of my daughter this minute.'

Abbey felt like a rag doll being tugged between arguing children. 'Let go of me, *all* of you!'

She struggled free and stood back a little to glare at them all. Blinking, she shook her head. 'This isn't happening; it really isn't.'

'You are *not* married, Abigail! You can't possibly be married. It's ridiculous.'

'You're right, it is ridiculous.' She laughed, a slightly manic sound, at her mother's outraged expression. 'But if what he says about not filing for divorce is true, then I am married. Although not for too much damn longer.'

Her eyes moved to Paul. 'I do need to talk to *you* about this and I am so sorry that you found out this way. It was a long time ago, when I was someone different. It doesn't matter, it really doesn't, Paul. I can fix this.'

'It doesn't matter?' Ethan asked sarcastically.

Anger rose inside her, mushrooming upward like a small atom bomb as she glared at him. From the moment she'd heard his voice behind her, her carefully planned life had started to fall apart. How dared he? How dared he just waltz back in and ruin everything? *Again.*

'You're damn right it doesn't matter. If it mattered so bloody much then you would have been here before now. You have no right to be here, Ethan, no right at all!'

'I have every right.'

Her anger transformed to tears. Hot, long-overdue tears that started low in her throat, choking her voice. 'No, you don't. You already ruined my life once and I won't let you do it again.'

His voice dropped huskily as he moved a step closer. 'I'm not here to ruin your life. I'm here because of your letter.'

'A letter I wrote to make sure you'd got a divorce!'

'So that you could marry this guy?' He jerked his head in Paul's direction.

'So I could get on with the rest of my life, yes.'

'If you want a divorce then just ask for one.'

She hesitated, searching his impassive face for something, but what? A hint that it wasn't what he wanted? Something that might tell her the reason he hadn't come back before now? Any sign of regret or of the same kind of pain she'd carried buried so well?

She saw nothing and her heart tore. It was ridiculous to have even looked. If he'd wanted her he'd have been there before now.

'I want a divorce.'

Ethan nodded. 'Fine.'

She watched as he turned and walked away through the sea of faces that was watching them. She even watched the sway of his broad shoulders as he left the room before her eyes came back to the people in front of her.

They all stared back at her. It was too much to deal with.

'I'm sorry.' She choked out the words. 'I'll explain, I promise. But not now.'

With a swift turn of her heel she spun round and marched across the room, pausing only long enough to grab a bottle of wine from the end of the buffet table.

CHAPTER TWO

'SO CAN we go home now?'

Ethan stared out of the hotel-room window to the green fields beyond. 'I don't know, Amy.'

'But she wants nothing to do with you. That should tell you something, shouldn't it?'

It should. But it wasn't enough. 'I need to know.'

Amy got up from the end of her bed and moved across to his side, waiting until he glanced over at her. 'I know you do. But this is history. I said that before we left home.'

He turned and smiled wryly at his childhood friend. Amy had stood by him through so much over the years and he appreciated that. Just as he appreciated her concern about his making this trip in the first place.

'I need to know.'

She stared into his eyes as he said the soft words. He knew she knew he needed to make sense of it all. It was what he'd been doing for years. Searching for explanations and trying to piece things back together. But at the same time, he knew she didn't want him in this place. This place that neither of them knew, where there was a good chance he could get hurt by someone who so obviously didn't give a damn any more.

'I know.' She squeezed his arm. 'So what do you want to do next?'

'I'm gonna go see her again.'

'And say what? She wants a divorce, Ethan. That letter was a goodbye, you said that yourself.'

'She can fill in the gaps for me. I need that time back.' He looked down at the faded photograph in his hand. It was all he had of her. A photograph with names scrawled on the back in his own handwriting: 'Ethan, A.J. and Jamie'. It was dated before his life had changed dramatically, and she'd been the only

thing he couldn't figure out. Until her letter came.

'Did you feel anything when you saw her?'

He shrugged. 'I don't know.' He smiled at
Amy again as he shrugged and repeated the
words: 'I *need* to know.'

It was the hangover from hell.

Not that drinking the wine had made everything go away for her. Hell, no. No such luck.
Forty-eight hours ago she'd been twenty-nine
and in control of her life.

Now she was thirty and her life was a big
bag of smelly stuff.

The missed calls on her mobile phone were
in double figures. Karyn had texted four times
and Abbey just knew when she eventually left
her room her mother would be waiting at the
foot of the stairs.

So she did what she'd done as a kid. Big
old country houses with notched cornerstones
had their advantages when it came to escaping
from a second-floor window. The ivy had

grown longer since her childhood, but she reckoned she'd manage somehow.

She just needed time on her own to deal with this stuff. To be strong enough to face all the people she'd lied to. Well, maybe 'lied' was a tad strong for her conscience to handle. 'Omitted to tell' felt vaguely better…

Ethan watched with amusement as she worked her way down the wall. Somehow it wasn't something he'd expected from the elegant woman he'd seen the night before.

He watched her denim-clad legs swing out of the window, watched her tentatively reach out for places to put her hands and feet. But mostly he got to watch her great rear work its way down the wall. Which helped greatly with his attention span. Every woman should look that good in jeans from the back. There should be a law written somewhere.

He continued to lean against the huge stone gatepost. Watched with a small smile as she landed neatly on her trainer-shod feet, wiped her hands down the front of her jeans and jogged down the lane with frequent backward glances.

As she got close she looked forward and stopped dead. Her eyes widened. She glanced back at the house, then back at him.

The devil and the deep blue sea.

Abbey watched as he unfolded his arms and leaned away from the gatepost. He started towards her. Oh, no. Not within eyesight of the occupants of the house!

She quickly stepped forward and grabbed the arm of his shirt, dragging him around the corner. 'Oh, no, you don't. I'm not having another argument with you in front of my mother.' She frowned. 'What are you doing here?'

'I wanted to talk. Don't they have doors in Ireland?'

She peeked around the gatepost again. 'I'm avoiding my mother.' *And half of the world.* Her head pounded and she let go of his sleeve to rub at her temples. 'You have no idea the mess you've made for me. You really don't.'

'We need to talk, A.J.'

Her heart caught again at the old nickname. He was the only one who had ever used it. She opened her mouth to speak and was distracted by movement at their side.

Mick Morrissey, local postman, grinned at them with crooked teeth. 'Mornin', Abbey, and this is your husband, isn't it?' He nodded at Ethan. 'You're welcome to Killyduff, Mr Wyatt. Nice to meet you.'

Ethan smiled with amusement. 'You too.'

Mick grinned at them both. 'It's a fine soft day today, isn't it?'

'Yeah, it is.'

Abbey shook her head. Which hurt more. 'Excuse us, Mick.' She reached for Ethan's sleeve again.

Ethan allowed her to pull him further up the small street. 'Everyone knows everyone here, don't they?'

'Yes, they damn well do.' She had no doubt that the entire town knew of Ethan's arrival by now and of who he was. It was a nightmare. 'Thanks to you I'm now hot news.'

He glanced at her as she moved them further from the town's main street. She wasn't hot news already?

Whatever other things he'd done in his life he'd sure as hell managed to marry a great-looking woman. Even the photograph hadn't done her justice.

Her dark hair was drawn back from her face in a pony-tail, showing the long length of her slender neck. And she had a gorgeous face, with even features and huge dark eyes. Eyes that glanced ahead and then back up at him.

He noticed the panic there as two elderly women smiled at them from a few steps away. Turning his arm slightly, he freed her grasp and enclosed her smaller hand in his. A glance through a gap in the hedgerow beside them revealed a small path to his inquiring eyes, so with a tug he pulled Abbey off the street and jogged them a few steps until they were beside a wide river.

She tugged her hand from his and stood facing him, her eyes searching his.

Even now looking at him could have her heart beating hard in her chest. How was that fair? He'd done it from the moment she'd met him.

'What?'

Abbey blinked at the softly spoken word, still mesmerized by his face. He was gorgeous. He'd always been gorgeous. Looking at him had been like a drug to her.

She let her eyes rove over him, from the top of his head and down over his face. His hair was still short, dark spikes appearing as a mizzle of rain fell on them. His face was still tanned from all the time he spent outdoors.

She did an inventory of all those things she'd once been so addicted to. His long lashes, the spark of light in his hazel eyes, his straight nose with the tiniest bump from where he'd broken it as a kid. Even his mouth still had that slight upward curve to it that hinted he was always smiling inside. Oh, yes, he was still a drug she could be addicted to. But like a reformed addict she had to resist the temptation.

Even as she'd searched his face for any obvious changes she could still somehow *feel* something different. 'You've changed.'

'Yes.' He nodded. 'I guess to what you remember I have. Older would be the first thing.'

'Me too.'

His eyes sparkled with the small smile that twitched his lips. 'I seem to recall a birthday party.'

Finally finding her spine, she managed to look away from him. 'Why are you still here? Wasn't making this much of a mess for me enough for you?'

'I didn't come to make a mess. I came to see you.'

Her laugh was sarcastic. 'Bit late, aren't you?'

'I'm sorry about that.'

'The time limit on sorry ran out around about seven years ago.'

If he was as awful a guy as she thought he was he'd have deserved the tone in her voice, but— 'A.J., there's something you need to know.'

'Something that will actually make a differ-ence?' Again she laughed. 'Oh, this should be good.'

He frowned and took a breath. 'I don't re-member you.'

'What do you mean, you don't remember me?' Her mind worked frantically with his words. 'If you don't remember me, then how are you even here? How did you know where to find me?'

'The letter.'

Her letter. The damned thing that had been so tough to write for so long, and that was supposed to have been the ending to things. Oh, yeah, look how well that had worked!

'The letter didn't tell you what I look like.' Abbey shook her head with a wry smile. 'You're a piece of work, Ethan Wyatt. I really don't know you at all, if that's the best you can come up with. Now, why are you *really* here?'

Ethan frowned at the glint in her eyes. He grew angry as she folded her arms across her chest. 'I sure as hell didn't come here to be judged.'

'You come marching into my home town with some lame-ass excuse for why I've been hanging for eight years and you'll bloody well get what you're given.'

'You've obviously not been hanging when you have a new fiancé at your heel.' He fought fire with fire. 'Or is that an acquisition you've made only recently?'

'That—' she tilted her head and smirked '—would be none of your business.'

They stared at each other as the river flowed by. Ethan took long deep breaths to calm his temper. He'd been trained to deal with trying situations, had been in a few dozen during his army career, but this was something new. Why *was* he so angry with her? It wasn't as if he'd not have felt the same way if the situation had been reversed. She had a right to be angry with him. And he had a right to, well, to what exactly? To be mad that she had a new fiancé? To care that this stranger hadn't tried to find out what had happened to him before now?

'Didn't you ever wonder why I disappeared? Want to know why I didn't come back after we'd obviously made a commitment to each other?'

Her throat threatened to close as he asked the question. Of course she had. Time and again. She'd waited for him for far longer than her common sense had told her to. But she wasn't about to share that information.

'It doesn't make any difference now, does it?' Again she smirked sarcastically. 'Especially not if you don't remember. I'm glad it was a memorable experience for you.'

He let her make it about two steps away from him when she turned to leave. 'Wait.'

Abbey stopped, but didn't turn.

'I had this.' He stepped closer and stretched his arm over her shoulder to hold his hand in front of her face.

She felt the warmth of his body close to her back and closed her eyes for a second as sensation swept over her. Then, slowly opening her eyes, she looked at the creased photograph. Her hand came up to take it from his long fingers as she looked down at the three smiling faces. 'It's us.'

His voice was low behind her. 'And Jamie.'

Jamie had been the third member of their inseparable trio that summer. Ethan's best friend.

Abbey's lips turned slightly upwards as she looked at them. Not that she didn't have dozens of similar photos hidden away in a box in her apartment. They all told the same story as this one and that memory made her smile for a brief second.

They'd just been so happy. So crazy and young. What had happened? Why hadn't things turned out as planned? Her voice was crackly. 'This was taken the day we went to Vegas.'

'The day we got married?'

'Yes.' She frowned again as she turned to look up at his face, closer to her than she'd expected. 'The day we got married. Why do you ask that like you don't know? You were *there*. We made those vows together.'

Ethan's eyes searched her face for long moments before he shook his head. 'I'm sorry, I don't remember that. I want to. I want to remember all of it, but I don't. That's why I'm here.'

'Why don't you just ask Jamie? He was your best man.'

'I can't.' He frowned hard. 'He's dead.'

Her eyes widened. *'What?'*

'If that date's right…?' One long finger pointed down at the digital date in a corner of the photo. He waited until she nodded. 'Then he died a few days after it was taken.'

'How?'

'A truck hit us. On the way back from the airport.'

The airport where they'd left her. To make the long trip home. To wait. Abbey's heart twisted painfully at the realization. Her last memories had been of that day. The three of them making the trip there filled with laughter and love. She'd played that day over and over in her mind for months, for longer than that…

'You were driving.' She remembered he'd driven all morning.

Ethan looked down, hiding his eyes from her. His voice completely deadpan, flat. As if he'd long since had to live with the facts he was now presenting to her. He answered with a nod. 'Yes. It hit Jamie's side and he died.'

'And you?'

He shrugged as he looked back into her eyes. 'I fought longer.'

There was no denying the honesty in his words. So matter-of-fact in the manner they were delivered. Abbey knew them to be true because Ethan had never lied to her. He'd been so up front with her from the start that it had almost scared her. Especially when it came to the depth of emotions he'd felt in such a short amount of time. But that honesty was why it had been so hard to accept that he would never come to get her when he'd promised to.

She studied him again. Then looked down at the photo in her hand. Then back up.

As he blinked back at her she could see questions forming in his eyes. 'I didn't know

I was supposed to come for you. I'm sorry about that.'

'You lost your memory?'

'Not all of it. I still remember everything else; growing up, family, friends, that kind of thing.'

'But not me.'

'No.' He smiled a wry smile. 'That was news.'

Unconsciously Abbey took a step back, realizing suddenly that it meant she was a stranger to him. A lump formed in her throat. 'Nothing at all? You don't remember that summer, meeting, falling in love?' *Making love?* The words got stuck in the region of her chest. All those things that had meant so much to her he didn't remember. Why? Why that and not anything else? 'All those things?'

Ethan took a step towards her, reaching out a large hand in her direction. 'I was hoping you'd tell me.'

She stared at his face, the face that had once smiled at her with all the love she could ever have wished for. She'd written the letter to let go. To have 'closure'. What he was saying meant that he'd had it, in a way, for a lot longer than her. Because to him it had never happened in the first place.

She placed the photo in his outstretched hand. 'I don't think I'm ready to deal with this right now.'

He watched as she backed away from him again. 'We need to talk about it, though. At least, I do. You have to understand that.'

'I do.' She nodded, her lower lip trembling slightly as she wrapped her arms around herself in a hug that didn't comfort any. 'Just not now, Ethan. I need to get my head round this.'

Ethan stood still. 'Soon, though.' The words were a statement rather than a question.

She nodded again. 'Soon.'

'I'm not leaving town 'til we do.'

CHAPTER THREE

KARYN stared at Abbey as she slumped onto the sofa at one end of her room. 'Where have you been? I've been texting you all morning.'

'I had to get out of the house.'

'I can imagine.' She flopped down beside her. 'Your mother has been prowling the halls looking for you.'

'I climbed out of the window.'

Karyn's eyes sparkled. 'You did what?'

Abbey shrugged. 'I always used to when I wanted to avoid her. My dad thought it was hilarious the first time he caught me at it. He had his own means of escape.'

Karyn stated the obvious. 'You're going to have to talk to her at some stage.' She added, 'And to Paul.'

Turning slightly, Abbey asked, 'You've talked to him?'

'Mmm.' Karyn glanced away. 'For a while last night and then this morning. He's a tad confused by all this.' She glanced back. 'Honey, we all are. You're *married*?'

'Yes.' She smiled wryly. 'And here's the kicker. To someone who doesn't remember being married.'

'How can he not remember something like that?'

'He was in a car accident.'

Karyn's jaw dropped, her elegant features transforming into a look of surprise. 'When?'

'The day he left me at the airport.' Abbey dropped her chin, twisting her cold hands together in her lap. 'I spent all this time wondering what had happened to him. Hating him for not coming back. And all that time he hadn't a clue who I was.' Her voice broke. 'And then there was Jamie.'

'Are you going to tell me you had a baby too?'

She glanced up at Karyn's wide eyes with a small sad smile. 'No. Being married was enough of a secret, don't you think? Jamie was Ethan's best friend. He died.'

'God. You knew him too?'

Abbey nodded. 'We spent all summer together.'

She still hadn't dealt with the fact that someone still so alive in her memory was gone now. She wouldn't ever bump into him somewhere or hear his voice. He'd been a pretty terrific guy. And he and Ethan had made up an irresistible duo. She'd never laughed again as much as she had that long summer.

Karyn sidled closer. 'Abbey, I know you had a life before I met you, but I had no idea all this stuff had happened. Why didn't you tell me?'

Wiping away the moisture from her cheeks, she shrugged. 'I didn't tell anyone. At the start because I thought Ethan would be here so we could explain it together. It just made perfect sense to us. But when he didn't come back I just felt that I couldn't confess how big a mistake I'd made.'

'You didn't try to find him?'

'I thought about it. Tried to. But I felt like a complete idiot. I was twenty-two years old, not exactly bursting with confidence, and I'd thought he loved me. I thought it would all be all right and we'd live happily ever after.' She laughed at her own *naïveté*. 'But things just aren't that simple, are they? And by the time I'd got angry enough to go find out what happened, my dad got sick.'

'And then he died.'

'And I was so upset I just couldn't think any more. And then it was too late, you know?'

'I know.' She nodded. 'But he's here now.'

'Only because I wrote a bloody letter.'

'Why?'

'Because I'd moved on!' She stood and began to pace in front of the sofa, her hands moving in the air beside her body. 'I'd met Paul and I'd made this great new life and I needed to make sure that I was free to make choices.'

'That closure thing.'

'Exactly.'

'That word has a lot to answer for.'

Abbey stopped in her tracks and looked down at her friend, her face sad. 'I'm sorry I didn't tell you. I wanted to so many times.'

Karyn smiled. She might consider herself shallow and materialistic, but deep down she had a heart the size of the island they lived on. 'I forgive you.'

Abbey smiled as she sat down again. 'Thanks.'

They both stared ahead for a while. Then Karyn took a breath. 'So do you still feel anything for him?'

'Ethan?'

'Yeah, that hot American you're technically still married to.'

'The one who doesn't even remember being married in the first place?'

'Yeah, that one. Unless there are more you want to tell me about.'

'No, one's enough.'

'I'd have thought so.' She smiled. 'So do you?'

Abbey searched her heart. 'He's still sexy as hell.'

'Oh, yes, that he is.'

'But I don't know anything about him now.'

'Any more than he does about you now.'

She nodded. 'Or about me from before, as it turns out.'

Karyn pursed her lips as she thought. 'In a bit of a quandary, then, aren't you? Are you still in love with him?'

Taking a deep breath, she answered as honestly as she could. 'I just don't see how love can survive all this.'

Ethan liked Killyduff. It was a bit like home. Everyone knew everyone else and smiled or said hello as he walked through the one street with stores it possessed. Only the odd thatched roof and the accents of the locals made it different from his home town in Connecticut.

Well, that, and the constant drizzle of rain that fell on his head.

He shoved his hands deep into the pockets of his jeans and wandered along the street. He'd never expected to be visiting a place like this, for a reason like this.

Why didn't he remember her?

It was a question that he'd asked himself time and time again since he'd got her letter. Surely something as important as falling in love and getting married should have stayed with him?

He could remember his social security number, his second grade teacher, all his friends and family. But not A.J. And not anything about that summer.

Why?

It made sense that he'd have wanted to block out the accident. That was only natural. He'd lost the best friend he'd ever had. And he still missed Jamie. Every damned day. Wondered at the fates that had taken his friend from him and chosen to have him stay despite how badly hurt he'd been. There had to have been a reason, didn't there? As someone who'd always carried the belief that there had to be a reason why things happened the way they did, he needed to hang onto the fact that there had to be something more he had to do. To achieve. Perhaps something left undone?

Like maybe the vows he'd not known he'd made.

His stomach growled at him. With a small frown of concentration he stopped in the middle of the street and looked down at his watch. Lunch already? His stomach growled again.

Ethan had always got hungry when things were difficult. He remembered *that*. Just as well that most things in his life were still within his control or he'd have weighed three hundred pounds by now.

An upward glance revealed a sign for the Fiddler's Elbow. A hostelry, according to the sign. He would be able to think better after something to eat, he reasoned, and then he would go and find A.J. again. At least that was a plan.

Once Abbey's eyes adjusted to the dim light inside the Fiddler's, she glanced around and wasn't overly surprised to find Ethan behind the bar.

'Oops.' Karyn grimaced beside her. 'Maybe a drink wasn't such a good idea, after all.'

The thought of a quick stop before facing Paul had seemed like a good idea. The thought that maybe she was turning into an alcoholic had crossed Abbey's mind, but Karyn had been adamant on the subject. Possibly something to do with the fact that she had become paler and paler as mid-afternoon had approached...

She stared at the scene in front of her. Ethan appeared to be having a great time. Damn him.

Like all small country pubs, the Fiddler's had its share of the usual customers planted around the edge of the large wooden bar. Nothing unusual there.

What *was* unusual was the assortment of brightly decked cocktail glasses they all appeared to be holding instead of their usual pint glasses.

Abbey blinked as Ethan shook a silver shaker in front of his wide chest. He was making *cocktails* for the locals?

'You want to go?' Karyn's voice sounded beside her again. 'Abbey?'

'Are those cocktails?'

'Yes, indeed. I do believe they are.'

Of course they were. Mesmerized, she approached the bar and asked the obvious. 'What are you doing?'

Ethan smiled a hundred-watt smile at her and her heart skipped a beat in her chest. Damn him.

'I'm introducing the guys here to some different flavours. You want one?'

'I'm having Sex at the Seaside.'

Abbey's eyes turned to Tom Flannery who was perched on his usual stool to her left. The man was a permanent fixture on that stool. Or at least had been since he'd retired. He had to be about eighty now.

'You mean Sex on the Beach, Tom.'

'Aye. That's it. But don't tell the wife.' He winked at her.

Abbey blinked back at him.

Ethan's deep voice interrupted her silence. 'Don't s'pose I can interest *you* in some Sex on the Beach, A.J.?'

Wide eyes shot to lock with his as he continued smiling. She read the challenge there and a long-hidden memory jumped into her mind. Her cheeks flamed.

Ethan's smile grew to a sexy grin as he poured his concoction into a tall glass in front of her. His voice dropped intimately. 'And I'm guessin' there's a story behind that look.'

Abbey glared at him.

'Yeah, thought so.' He pushed the glass towards her, his voice dropping intimately. 'Maybe you'll tell me about it some time.'

She dragged her eyes from his to focus on the glass. With a frown she admitted to herself there was no way in hell she could tell him about that particular memory. Somehow describing something so private to someone who was technically a stranger was just too invasive to her. The Ethan she'd known had been right there. Sharing the intimate experience with her.

'I don't think so.'

Ethan knew she was referring to something other than the drink in front of her. 'Perhaps I could mix something else for you.'

She looked back at him with a raise of one dark eyebrow. 'I can mix myself something.'

His mouth twitched. 'Why mix alone when we could mix together?'

Because look where that got me last time. She managed not to voice the answer aloud. Instead she raised her chin a visible inch and leaned closer to him. 'You still remember the whole cocktail-making routine, then, I take it?'

Not entirely managing to convince himself that he had been talking about cocktails, Ethan merely quirked an eyebrow. 'I made extra money in college with this routine.'

'I know.'

Of course she did. He watched with guarded eyes as she lifted a section of bar and joined him behind the wooden surface. 'What are you doing?'

'Mixing something, apparently.' Karyn grinned as she approached the opposite side of the bar.

Ethan aimed a smile in her direction. 'Does this kind of stuff much, does she?'

'Oh, you know, just…never.' Karyn continued grinning as she pulled up a stool, propped her elbow on the bar and rested her chin in her hand. 'I for one can't wait.'

'So.' Abbey walked up to Ethan and lifted a bottle, twirling it in a manner that would have made a cowboy with a six-shooter proud. 'Sex on the Beach, wasn't it?'

'Yes, ma'am, indeed it was.'

She nodded with a half-smile and then threw the twirling bottle in his direction. With a flick of his wrist Ethan caught the bottle in mid-spin and slammed it down on the bar. 'If we're gonna do this, then we need to get ourselves ready.'

'Very important thing, preparation.'

His smile grew as he played along with her game. Or was it his game? As they moved in the small space behind the bar, setting out glasses and ingredients, the boundaries somehow became blurred to him.

'Knowing what you're doing certainly helps.'

'Mmm.' Abbey leaned past him, her arm brushing against the wall of his chest. 'Experience counts.'

He smiled down at her with a glint in his eyes as the final ingredient was put in place. His voice dropped to a low drawl. 'New experiences can be interesting too.'

Karyn listened to their words and read the innuendo. 'Enough with the foreplay. We're ready for a show here.'

Tom Flannery laughed loudly and a small crowd gathered round as music played from the jukebox in the background.

'You ready?'

Abbey smiled a slow smile at Ethan's soft words. He might not have remembered the scene they were playing out, but she did. And reliving the memory felt good.

'I'm ready.'

Lifting a bottle, she began to spin it again as she turned towards the audience. 'In life it's important to always get the right mix of ingredients.'

As she flicked the bottle in the air she spun out of Ethan's way and he reached up to catch the bottle with an arch of his arm. 'Too much of one thing can do you no good, that's for sure.'

Abbey reached round him and dropped the open shaker on the bar in time to catch the liquid as Ethan poured it. She winked at Karyn. 'But mixed with the right things it can be *awful* good.'

Ethan picked another bottle and spun it upward for Abbey to catch as he stepped back. 'You just need to get the mix right.'

They both picked up bottles and spun them simultaneously, their bodies moving in a synchronicity born of familiarity. 'In order to make things work…'

The bottles switched hands in mid-air and then Abbey did a spin out of Ethan's way so he could place the lid on the shaker. '…the way they should do.'

He spun the shaker into the air for Abbey to catch and shake in front of her body. 'You get the mix right…'

He leaned over her shoulder to throw ice in a glass, his voice close to her ear. '...and things work out so much better...'

Abbey leaned back against him slightly as his arms snaked around her waist to place a small umbrella and a long straw in the glass as she finished pouring. '...than you could ever have imagined.'

Ethan felt her lean against him as she finished pouring. Watched as she tilted her head into his shoulder to look up at him with a smile. And it seemed the most natural thing in the world to kiss her.

CHAPTER FOUR

IT WAS as if the last eight years had never happened.

The time rolled away as Ethan's warm mouth settled on Abbey's. Her hand reached up to curve around his chin, her fingertips brushing against the suggestion of coarse stubble she found there.

This was what her heart had found so hard to let go of. This thrill. This jolt to her toes of pure sensation as his mouth moved with hers.

Ethan.

He was here. Not some distant memory or some hot night-time dream. He was here. And he was kissing her. Kissing her the way he used to.

She frowned slightly and managed to drag her lips from his to look up into his eyes.

He looked back at her, his eyes dark as his mind worked. Then, with applause and whistles in the background for their floor show, he asked her in a low voice meant only for her ears, 'Is this how it was with us?'

A lump formed in her throat at the question. 'Yes.'

'Then I think I understand a little better.'

They stared at each other while Karyn reached for the glass they had just poured. She smiled as she sipped from the straw, then allowed her eyes to glance round the smiling faces. Until she looked slightly behind her at the one face that wasn't smiling.

'Abbey?'

Abbey's eyes remained fixed on Ethan's. 'Yes?'

'Uh, *Abbey*.'

She managed to drag her eyes away to look at her friend, whose tone had become more demanding of attention. 'What?'

'Paul's here.'

'That was quite a floor show you both put on in there.' Paul glanced at her with a frown as they walked along the main street. 'I hadn't realized you were such an exhibitionist.'

She wasn't. At least, she hadn't been in a very long time. But they both knew that Paul was familiar with the new, improved Abbey.

'I'm not usually. You know that.'

He smiled slightly. 'I thought I knew a lot of things about you.'

'You did.' She corrected herself when she used the past tense. 'You do, Paul. You know me now. The person I am *now*. Not the girl that married Ethan.'

Paul stopped and turned to look down at her, his blue eyes searching her face. 'And which one was that I just saw in the bar?'

Good question. She thought over her answer carefully as she looked up at him. This great guy she'd been seeing for months now. The one that cared enough about her to want to get married. She knew he deserved better.

'I guess it's hard not to slip back into an old habit.'

'Are you still in love with him, Abbey?'

It was the million-dollar question. 'I loved him when I married him. But that was a long time ago. I don't even know him now.'

'What happened?'

'That's a long story.'

He blinked as he looked at her. 'I have time.'

It was just typical of him. Even now when he should have been mad as hell, he was still taking the time to let her explain it. Explain why she had felt the need to keep such a big secret from him while he had been prepared to make such a big commitment to her. She felt lower than a snake's ass.

'You really are a great guy.'

Paul grimaced slightly at the statement. 'That's one of those things a woman says just before she tells the guy she's dumping him.'

Abbey continued looking up at him.

'Is that what you're doing?' He stepped closer to her as people bumped past them on the pavement. 'You want me to just disappear?'

Was that what she wanted? Was she prepared to just throw away all of the new life she'd built for herself over one crummy cocktail routine? She frowned as she thought about all the things she'd worked so hard for. About the relationship she had with Paul now. He really was a great guy. They didn't just appear every day. She knew that much.

'I think this is just going to take some time to sort out, is all.'

'Is it?' His expression told her he wasn't quite convinced of that. 'I know you and I haven't exactly been love's young dream—'

'We've talked about that before and that's not what either of us is looking for in our lives now.'

'Maybe not.'

Her eyebrows rose. 'But I think we've built a relationship, don't you?'

'That word can cover a lot of things these days.'

Yes, it could. And it wasn't the case that theirs had been the whirlwind she'd experienced before. But that whirlwind of the past hadn't lasted. Fate had decided that with no input on her behalf. This time she could do something about it, couldn't she? She could fight to hang onto what she had.

'If you want to disappear, I'll understand.'

Paul thought for a moment, then smiled softly. 'I'm not sure I'm ready to do that.'

Abbey let her breath out in a small sigh. At least there was one constant in her life that she could rely on. He really did have the patience of a saint.

'I don't really deserve that.'

'I'm not a quitter, Abbey. You know that about me from working with me at least.' He stepped even closer and lifted his hands to cup her elbows. 'You sort out a divorce with this guy and we'll take it from there. Okay?'

She nodded with a tiny smile as he drew her close and enfolded her in his arms. As she rested her head against his shoulder her voice was muffled, hiding a slight tremor in its tone. 'Okay.'

'So that's her fiancé, then.' Ethan leaned his forearms on the bar opposite Karyn as Abbey left with Paul.

He hadn't wanted her to leave. It was the weirdest sensation. Half of him had just wanted to hold onto her and not let her leave the space beside him. A complete stranger. One he'd barely met and already he felt the need to be possessive of her company? Weird.

Karyn studied his face for a second before sipping through her straw and shrugging. 'She hasn't said yes.'

'Why not?'

'You'd have to ask Abbey that one.'

He raised a dark eyebrow. 'She just left. In case you hadn't noticed.'

'And that bugs you, does it?' She twirled her straw around, tinkling ice against the glass.

Ethan considered lying for a split second before smiling. 'Apparently so.'

'And why would that be, do you think?'

He leaned back and began to tidy away some of the cocktail equipment behind the bar. 'Damned if I know.'

'Because you don't remember her.'

He stopped what he was doing to stare her straight in the eye. 'You think I'm lying about that?'

Karyn looked straight back at him.

'You do, don't you?'

She shrugged in an 'I dunno' kind of way.

Ethan swore. He tidied away the remaining bottles with a couple of slams before turning on her with, 'Why the *hell* would I do that?'

Karyn sighed. 'Maybe when you saw her you realized you'd made a mistake and this was the best way you could think of to get out of it.'

His expression was stunned. 'What the hell kinda guys you dealing with over here?'

'Now, you see, that'd be a long story.'

'Well, where I come from people don't pull lousy stunts like that. If I'd screwed up that bad, then I'd stand up and say so. I wouldn't hide behind a lie.'

'That's very honourable.'

'Yes, it damn well is. Because—' he suddenly realized he didn't even know her name '—*lady*, that's the way I am and I'm not about to apologize for that. You can think what you want, but all I know is six months ago I got a letter outta the blue from some woman who's been a face in a photograph to me for eight years. If I'd loved someone enough to damn well marry them, I'd never have let them go.'

With a swift turn he lifted the bar's hatch and stepped past Karyn just as Tom Flannery reappeared from the toilets. 'You away, Ethan?'

Ethan stopped to smile. 'Yeah, Tom, I am. You look after that hip, you hear.'

'I will.' Tom rubbed a hand at his left hip. 'I'll try them there things you said to ease it. And you can make me Sex at the Seaside any time. Can't hardly feel the pain.'

Ethan grinned. 'It's a miracle.'

'Aye, you got to watch them miracles. Never know where they appear.'

'Bye, Tom.'

Karyn's eyes met Ethan's again before he frowned and marched towards the door. She sighed, then lifted her bag and slipped off the stool to follow him. Her hand touched his by the door. 'Ethan, wait.'

'What?'

'Firstly, it's Karyn.' She reached her hand out to shake his. 'I like to consider myself Abbey's best friend. I thought I knew her better than anyone else 'til you came along.'

Ethan ignored her hand and looked at her with guarded eyes. 'So this is what, the protective act?'

'Possibly.' She dropped the hand. 'But you've got to admit this is a little out of the ordinary.'

He brushed his fingers back through his short hair, looking at the door for a moment as he thought. Then he glanced down at her. 'I didn't come halfway across the world to lie, Karyn.'

'So what *did* you come for?'

Initially he'd just made the trip for answers. Had reasoned with himself that one trip would fill in the blanks that had tortured him for so long. But in an extremely short space of time he found he had a different answer to her question.

'I came to get to know my wife.'

'To find out if you still love her?'

He looked at the door again. 'Maybe to find out why I loved her enough to get married to her.'

'You haven't considered getting married since your accident?' Karyn raised an eyebrow at his profile. 'Eight years is a long time to not get involved with anyone.'

Ethan shrugged as he glanced back at her again. 'Nothing that serious. I guess I thought I was a confirmed bachelor.'

She laughed. 'Apparently not.'

He managed a smile as he pushed the door open onto the street. 'So it would seem.'

Karyn followed him when he held the door open for her, turning to face him again as the door closed behind them. 'Abbey didn't get involved with anyone for a long time either. I always thought it was just because she was so career orientated. But maybe there was another reason.'

He smiled at her words of encouragement then glanced over her head to the couple down the pavement from them. 'Well, whatever her reason was, she's sure as hell involved now, isn't she?'

Karyn turned and looked to where Paul was drawing Abbey into his arms. She grimaced as she looked back at Ethan. 'Life is never simple.'

Ethan couldn't drag his eyes away from them. His gut twisted at the sight. What right had he to walk in and take that away from her? Maybe he'd been wrong to make the trip, after all. It had been selfish. To walk on in and complicate this stranger's life. Maybe he should just give her a divorce and leave her to make a life with someone else. That would be the logical thing to do. The sensible and right thing. And Ethan had always tried to do the right thing, hadn't he?

Hazel eyes glanced down at the woman in front of him. 'Thanks for the talk, Karyn.' He reached out his hand to shake hers. 'It was real nice to meet you.'

'You too, Ethan.' She held onto his hand for a moment. 'But I wouldn't run off too fast if I were you.'

He raised an eyebrow in question. 'You think?'

Nodding, she released his hand and glanced back over her shoulder again. 'You both need some kind of closure to this. Abbey as much as you. And you have to remember she's had more time than you to torture herself over this.'

CHAPTER FIVE

'HE'S a great guy.'

'Who is?'

Karyn flopped onto the end of Abbey's bed as she changed after a shower. 'Your husband.'

'You spent time with him?' She stared at her friend's reflection in her dresser mirror.

Karyn lay across the bed, bending an elbow to prop her head on an outstretched hand. 'We chatted a while after you left the bar with Paul.'

Abbey's eyes narrowed slightly. 'Oh, really?'

'Uh-huh. I still stand by my original observation that he's hot too.'

Abbey took a breath and lifted her brush from the glass surface to drag it through her hair. 'Well, maybe you should still make a play for him, then.'

Karyn noticed the edge to her voice and smiled. 'Oh, yeah, because you'd be fine with that, wouldn't you?'

'No, actually, I wouldn't.'

'Because I'm your best friend or because it's Ethan?'

She stopped smoothing her hair and turned round on her stool. 'Karyn, are you telling me you fancy Ethan?'

'No.'

'Then what exactly are you saying?'

'I'm just pointing out the fact that he's a great guy and pretty damn hot.' She shrugged while continuing to smile. 'I'm just stating the obvious.'

'Yes, because obviously I'd never have known those things before. What with having married him and all.'

'So you still fancy him, then?'

'What kind of question is that?'

Another shrug. 'A fairly simple one. Do you or don't you still fancy the guy you're married to?'

Abbey stood up and walked to her wardrobe. 'This is a pointless conversation.'

'Only for as long as you keep running away from the answers.'

'Oh, for crying out loud!' She spun round to glare at her friend. 'What do you want me to say? I know he was a great guy eight years ago and I know that he hasn't changed that much on the outside and I fancied him like all hell the first time I clapped eyes on him. What more do you want? It still doesn't mean I'd change anything now.'

Karyn blinked. 'So you're going to marry Paul, then.'

'I can hardly marry Paul when I'm still married to Ethan. There's a law.'

'So you're going to see Ethan again?'

Abbey sighed and threw her arms in the air. 'It'll be a bit bloody difficult to get a divorce without seeing him again, won't it?'

'And you're quite certain a divorce is what you want?'

The question stopped her in her tracks. Dropping her chin, she looked at her bare feet for several long seconds before looking back at Karyn with a wry smile. 'It just wouldn't work, even if Ethan still remembered. I have a life now and I'm sure he does too. And they're far apart.'

Karyn wriggled into a sitting position. 'People change their lives to be with other people all the time.'

'Not ones that have worked as hard to get where they are as I have. And I'm fairly sure that Ethan isn't about to give up his career to move to dear old Ireland.'

'How do you know that? And there's no way you can say you couldn't have a great career in America. They love Irish people there.' Karyn's face became animated as she warmed to her subject.

'*If* he even wanted to…' She shook her head. 'I couldn't wait for him again. Been there, done that. And he never came.'

Karyn pointed out the obvious, again. 'He's here now.'

'Out of curiosity, I'd say. Wouldn't you want to see what I was like if you didn't remember me?'

'He obviously remembers some things.' She pursed her lips slightly before continuing. 'Or was that kiss just part of the cocktail-making routine?'

It had been. The repartee had changed each time they'd done it; there was nothing out of the ordinary there. But the kiss? No one had forced him to kiss her. No one had forced her to enjoy it.

With a glance at her feet again, she frowned as she thought. 'I guess he just got caught up in the moment.'

Karyn watched as she turned back to the wardrobe and rummaged through her clothes. Having walked with Ethan for nearly half an hour she'd taken strongly to him. And it had struck her that he was much more what she would have pictured for Abbey than Paul was. Paul was just so controlled, cautious almost. As if he held a part of himself back. And Karyn had never seen anything to indicate that he was any different with Abbey. It bugged her about him. And somehow she'd always felt that the overly careful Abbey needed more than that.

'Was that how it started with you two?'

Abbey tried hard to focus on the clothes in front of her. But already her mind was picturing a different time. Ethan had flirted with her for weeks when she'd first arrived at the kids' camp that summer. At first it had been flattering, but she'd thought nothing of it. Summer romances never lasted, after all. Particularly when they were half a world away from her reality.

But when Ethan set his mind to something he was extremely determined. He'd continued to charm her on a daily basis until she'd later joked he'd just plain worn her down. And then the fun had really begun...

She'd been head over heels in the blink of an eye.

Her memory filled in the moment he'd first kissed her. But even though it brought a smile to her lips, like every memory she had it also brought a stab of pain that it hadn't worked.

'It doesn't matter how it started. The fact is that things didn't work out. It's over and done with.'

'That kiss in the bar said different.'

'That kiss was spur of the moment. It doesn't mean anything.'

'You mean you're trying to convince yourself it doesn't mean anything,' Karyn persisted. 'You have to remember something, though. It may have been an old habit that *you* slipped into. But Ethan doesn't remember. So he kissed you because he wanted to. Simple attraction.'

Abbey's breath caught and she turned on her heel to stare at her smug-faced friend. 'What?'

'No one forced him to kiss you, sweetie.'

Abbey continued to stare.

Karyn continued with a shrug. 'If you're a stranger to him, then he kissed you because he wanted to. Not because it was an old habit *he* was slipping into.'

Her train of thought caught Abbey completely off guard. She had thought about the kiss for half the afternoon. The heat of it still tingling on her lips even as they spoke. But she had told herself it was just a case of their history spilling over into the present. A little 'slip up', of sorts.

But what Karyn said was true. If Ethan didn't remember that history, then why had he kissed her?

'Gotcha on that one, haven't I?'

Abbey's wide eyes stared across the room.

'It hadn't occurred to you, had it?'

'No.'

Karyn nodded. She'd thought as much. 'Hon, I really think you need to have a proper talk with him before you go ambling off into the sunset with Paul.'

'Paul's a great guy.'

'Yeah, I know. You keep saying.'

Abbey frowned. 'Because it's bloody well true! You tell me one other guy that would have taken this whole secret-husband thing as well as he has.'

'That's a point in his favour, all right.'

Abbey turned and dragged a dress from the wardrobe, smoothing the soft material with one hand as she checked for creases. 'Ethan is my past.'

Karyn had to strain to hear the softly spoken words. She took a breath before speaking again. 'Maybe. But I for one would find it tough to move on from here if I didn't have that damned closure you looked for in your letter. You need to spend some time with him to make sure you're not making a mistake letting him go.'

Abbey continued to hold the dress up as she turned her head. 'There's nothing to let go of. Ethan being married to me is a piece of paper to him. He doesn't remember the things I do.'

'The memories may be gone, but that doesn't mean the feelings have.'

'The one goes hand in hand with the other.'

'Maybe.' Karyn stood up and walked towards the doorway, turning as she pulled the door open. 'But maybe not.'

Her hand hesitated a few inches from the door. What was she *doing*?

She could have just picked up the phone and talked to him that way. It would have been easier. Simpler. It would have highlighted the yellow streak down her spine, but she could have lived with that...

Before she could make the decision to walk away, the door opened and she found herself on eye-level with a blonde-haired woman.

The woman's eyes widened in surprise. 'Hi.'

'Hello.' Abbey stunned herself with her own sparkling conversation. 'I was looking for Ethan Wyatt.'

'He's taking a shower.'

Was he indeed? Her eyes glanced past the woman to the unmade bed and her furtive imagination kicked into overdrive. 'I see.'

'He won't be long, if you want to wait.'

'No, I don't think so—' She stepped back from the door and then her eyes fell on an almost naked Ethan in the background.

'Thought you'd gone to get food...' He looked up, the towel he was using to dry his hair going still in his hand. 'A.J.'

Abbey's dark eyes locked with his over the woman's shoulder. 'Ethan.'

He dropped the hand rubbing his hair to his side and smiled. 'I didn't expect to see you so soon.'

Obviously not. She quirked an eyebrow as anger spiralled deep in her stomach. She had no right to be angry that she'd found him with another woman. But the feeling was there nevertheless. Damn him.

'It was a spur-of-the-moment decision, believe me.' She glanced at the other woman again before looking back at him. 'I'll come back some other time.'

Ethan moved forward when she stepped away from the door. 'No, wait. Come on in. Amy was just going out.'

Amy stepped to one side. 'Yes, I was. And I know Ethan wants to talk to you, so, please, do come in.'

Abbey hesitated, blinking as she thought. She wasn't at all comfortable with having called to 'visit' when they'd obviously been busy beforehand. Or maybe 'getting busy' would have been a better way to put it.

'Please?'

She looked at him as he spoke, his eyes sparkling at her. Her conversation with Karyn might have been the catalyst to her decision to come and talk to him, but this little scene had just made her all the more determined to get things over and done with.

With a slight rise of her chin she smiled sweetly at Amy as she stepped past her. 'Thank you.'

Amy merely nodded and stepped into the hallway, pausing only to glance at Ethan before she closed the door.

Ethan waited patiently until she looked him in the eye. Which took a moment or two as her eyes moved over his naked body above the towel wrapped around his waist. She flushed slightly when she saw he'd watched her looking.

'Maybe you should get dressed.'

'Maybe I should.'

The flush grew warmer across her cheeks. 'I can wait.'

Ethan's smile grew into a lazy, sexy grin that Abbey remembered only too well from the moments after they'd made love. She knew that spark in his eyes too. The unspoken suggestion that said he was well aware of his own state of undress and how it was affecting her.

'It's mild enough. I won't catch a chill, if that's what's worrying you.'

That thought hadn't worried her in the least. What worried her, no, scratch that, what *irritated* her, was that she was so affected by his semi-naked body that her own body seemed prepared to forget the fact that another woman had just left the room.

'I would be more comfortable if you would get dressed.'

'Don't married people get to see each other undressed in this country?'

She stepped back as he stepped towards her. 'Married people who see each other more than once every eight years probably do. But I'm a stranger to you, remember?'

'I've been looking at that picture of you for years now. You're not exactly a stranger.'

That stopped her for a second, her eyes questioning. 'Well, you can't say I'm a wife to you, either.'

Ethan shrugged his broad, naked shoulders. 'In the eyes of the law I can.'

The shrug brought her traitorous eyes back to the wide expanse of his chest and down over what she knew in the modern world as his 'six pack'. He did have a *great* six pack.

Her throat went dry. Shaking her head to get back into reality, she squared her shoulders and looked back into his grinning face.

'That's what I'm here to talk about.'

Ethan quirked an eyebrow. 'Is it?' He moved closer to her. 'Or is it that you haven't been able to forget about that kiss this afternoon any more than I have?'

CHAPTER SIX

'OH, YOU'RE just something special, aren't you?'

The grin remained on Ethan's face as he continued to step towards Abbey. 'You obviously thought so once.'

'I was practically a child then!' She watched his slow approach with suspicious eyes. 'I've done a hell of a lot of growing up since and I can see you for exactly what you are now.'

The grin faded. 'Oh, really? And what might that be?'

Folding her arms across her breasts, she tilted her head to one side and smiled sarcastically. 'Someone who quite obviously thinks they're God's gift, for one thing.'

He stood a little taller on his bare feet. 'And you've gotten that assumption from where, exactly?'

'From the fact that you're flirting with me when your girlfriend has barely had time to get down the hallway!'

His hazel eyes blinked at her for a few moments, long dark lashes brushing against his tanned skin, and then the spark returned and he smiled. 'You're jealous.'

'I am not.'

'Yeah, you are.' He continued to step towards her. 'And you just hate that, don't you?'

'Like I said—' She glanced from side to side, suddenly aware that he was backing her into a corner. Literally. 'God's-gift syndrome.'

'No.' He said the word slowly as he stepped close enough to block her from escape. Then he waited for a second, his voice dropping intimately. 'You see, I know how that emotion feels, A.J.'

Abbey stared up at him, her breathing suddenly laboured.

'I know, 'cos that's how *I* felt when I saw you with your boyfriend.'

The air seemed to crackle between them as his soft words sank slowly into her brain. He was jealous? How could he be jealous?

'You don't remember.' The words came in a hoarse whisper. 'So how can you feel that?'

'Damned if I know.'

Her breasts continued to rise and fall as her heart beat an erratic rhythm. 'I can't do this again.'

'Kiss me?'

That *wasn't* what she'd been referring to, but her eyes automatically travelled to the sensual curve of his mouth. She'd been thinking about that kiss entirely too much. And of all the ones in the past that had preceded it. If it came to a choice she was quite sure she *could* kiss him again. But that was one of the many things she had to avoid.

'I can't get involved with you again.'

'Because of Paul?' He asked the question with a frown.

'Because of Paul, because of Amy. Because remembering you and me still hurts.' The confession came out in a rush. Revealing more than she'd ever intended when she'd made her way to his room. But it was out now.

She looked up into his eyes and took a breath. 'I can't do this again.'

Ethan stared down at her and could read the pain in her eyes without even trying. She had stunning eyes. Dark depths that he was quite sure he could have spent hours getting lost in. Forgetting about his life, the past he didn't remember. It would have been easy to just give in to the longing he seemed to feel in his gut when he looked into those eyes.

But surely it was easier on them both to let go of it? He could just let her believe the incorrect assumption she'd made about his relationship with Amy. He could set her free and let her have a life with Paul. Couldn't he? Or, more to the point—shouldn't he?

He reached out a hand and brushed his fingers down through the long hair that lay against her shoulder. 'If I'd known about us I'd have come back before now.'

Abbey smiled a soft, sad smile. 'I always thought so. But you didn't and neither of us can fix that now.'

His hand stilled. 'Can't we?'

She reached up for his hand and placed it back at his side, following the movement with her eyes before she looked back at him. 'No, Ethan, we can't.'

He studied her face again for a long moment before taking a step back from her. Turning to walk towards the windows, he ran a hand through his damp hair.

All of his life he'd tried to do the right thing. To be honourable. Living with that code had allowed him to hold his head high. To have pride in what he did. But for the first time in his life he wasn't ready to do what was right.

'I'm not ready to give this up.'

'What?' She stared in shock at his naked back. 'What do you mean you're not ready? Ethan, you're with someone else! *I'm* with someone else!'

'Are you?' He turned to look back at her. 'Then why haven't you said yes to him?'

'Because I'm still married to you!'

'Is that the only reason?'

'He happens to be a great guy!' She angered herself with how easily the overused phrase jumped out of her mouth.

Ethan's face grew dark as he stepped towards her again. 'If he's such a damn great
guy, then how come you didn't tell him about
me?'

Her mouth opened, but words didn't come
out.

Ethan continued back to her corner of the
room. 'Could it be that maybe you didn't tell
him because you weren't ready to let go?'

'I wrote a letter to let go. I should have written it years ago.'

'But you didn't.'

She tried to sidestep out of the dangerous
corner, but was immediately held back by
Ethan's hand on her forearm. He leaned closer,
his breath teasing the hair across her forehead.
'You didn't because you still wanted me to
come back.'

Tugging at her arm only increased the pres-
sure of his hold on her. 'You *still* haven't come
back. Because the person I was in love with
isn't a part of you any more.'

The words stung. He stared down at her
with angry eyes. 'That time was taken from

me, Abbey. I had no say in it. You think I asked to have that truck hit us? You think I asked for all those long months in a hospital? You think I wanted Jamie gone?'

She'd never seen such a look of anguish on Ethan's face before. The pain so palpable she could almost feel it herself. With a step that brought her body close to his naked chest, she looked up at him. 'I don't think any of those things, but I can't make it right for you either.'

'Can't you?' His voice softened in response to the softness of hers, his vice-like grip on her arm easing until his thumb was rubbing back and forth against her skin. 'You can't bring Jamie back, but you can give me those missing months. I need them back.'

Dark hair fell off her shoulder in a silent whisper as she tilted her head and searched his eyes. 'That's why you're here? So that I can give you back the memories?'

He looked down at the red marks he'd left on her arm and frowned at his own negligence. She didn't deserve his anger. It wasn't her who had done the damage, after all. All she'd done was wait for him. And get hurt in the process.

He let go of her arm.

Abbey didn't move. Couldn't while her mind was working so hard and her chest hurt so bad. 'Would knowing make it better for you?'

His naked shoulders shrugged again. 'I don't know that it would. But I can't keep walking around feeling like six months of my life was stolen from me.'

Abbey knew how that must feel. Because she'd felt that way for eight years. As if all she'd dreamed of and wanted so badly had been stolen from her. It had hurt beyond words. Listening to Ethan saying the same thing made it hurt again.

She couldn't fix what had happened, but maybe she could take some of his pain away. Because it was obvious how much he still hurt. And the part of her that had loved him so very much couldn't let him feel that way.

'Okay.'

His eyes shot to meet hers. 'Okay?'

She nodded, rubbing absently at her arm. 'Okay. I'll tell you everything you want to know, but then you have to do something for me in return.'

'Like what?'

She squared her shoulders and raised her chin. 'You have to give me a divorce and leave.'

He frowned at her words.

Her tongue moved over dry lips. 'And never come back.'

'You okay?'

Abbey blinked at Paul across the table. She had thought she could handle a short visit with Ethan before she met him for dinner in the hotel dining room. She hadn't planned for how complicated it would be.

'I'm fine.'

He looked at her as if he didn't quite believe that, but then smiled and let it pass. 'So what do you want to eat, then?'

The very thought of eating turned her stomach in a million different directions. She let her eyes glance over the menu for a while, then set it on the table in front of her before looking up into Paul's face. Her breasts rose against the scooped neck of the dress as she took a breath. 'I've been thinking.'

Paul nodded as if he'd suspected as much. 'And?'

'Maybe you should go back to Dublin for a while.'

'Without you, you mean?'

'Yes.'

He set his own menu down and searched her face as she avoided his intense stare. 'For how long, exactly?'

She glanced back down at the tabletop. 'I don't know.'

A frown creased his forehead. 'Give me an idea. I need to know for work purposes at the very least.'

'I'm not quitting.'

He waited until she looked back at him again, the frown still in place. 'Not quitting your job or not quitting on you and me?'

'On either, I hope.' She meant the words. She had no intention of giving up on the things that she'd worked so hard for.

'Is he staying here too?'

It didn't take her to be a mind-reader to work out who he meant. 'Yes. For a while.'

Paul's frown grew and he leaned back a little from her. 'I see.'

'I doubt that.' Abbey wasn't entirely sure she 'saw' herself. But now, filling in those gaps for Ethan was almost like a 'to do' list that had to be completed to allow her to move on with the rest of her life. 'I asked him for the divorce, Paul. It just needs a little time to sort through, is all.'

Noises from the half-full dining room filtered around them as Paul mulled over her words, studied her face. Then with a breath he leaned forward, his voice low. 'And where does that leave us while you sort these things?'

It was a good question.

'I just need some time. A little space. And hopefully we'll be exactly where we were before.'

'And where *is* that, Abbey?'

She blinked as she looked into his eyes. In their blue depths she could see questions, and maybe even a flicker of hope? He'd given her time to think over his proposal. Been as patient with her answer to it as he had been the whole way through their relationship. But she knew she'd been holding back from making a firm commitment to him.

'You've been very patient with me.'

'We were both fairly sick of the dating game before we met.' He smiled encouragingly. 'Taking it the old-fashioned route worked for us both.'

It had been perfect, in fact. She smiled back at him. 'Yes, it did. And I'm still not running out on you. But it's only fair I sort out all this mess for both of us. I can't ask you to wait around while I do that. It wouldn't be fair.'

'Is he still in love with you?'

'No.' Her answer was quick and accompanied by a wry twist of her mouth. 'You have nothing to worry about there. He has a new girlfriend.'

'Is she here?'

'Yes.'

Paul seemed to think over her words for a moment as he leaned back in his seat again. He looked around the room for a few seconds, then shrugged as he said, 'I do have to be back in the office tomorrow.'

They were both supposed to have been. But who could have known that the birthday week-end could turn out so complicated? Abbey sure as hell hadn't.

'And you should go. They need you there.'

'And you don't need me here.'

'I guess I don't need anything more difficult than this already is.'

He nodded. 'I suppose it's easier for you to ask me to go than it is for you to ask him.'

His statement was true. And Abbey felt a pang of guilt. Because, after all, Paul hadn't asked for her to hold back from him and it was what she'd been doing ever since she'd started going out with him. She'd held back her past, held back a part of herself that had been stung so badly by that past, and she knew he deserved better than that.

'I have as much talking to do with you as I have with him. But I can't do that until he's gone—surely that makes sense?'

His mouth turned upwards a barely perceptible amount. 'The lesser of two evils, huh?'

'I can't make a commitment to you with all this stuff hanging in the air. I'm sorting it out, Paul, really I am. I just need to do it one step at a time.' She looked down at the now-familiar tabletop as she formed the words in her mind. This was what the new, improved Abbey had done for all these years now. She had taken control and tidied every part of her life into neat compartments. This just happened to be the one compartment she'd left untouched. It was a simple, matter-of-fact kind of thing. That was all. 'I'll understand if you don't want to wait around.'

'You know where I'll be, Abbey. I'll leave it to you to come to me. At least that way I'll always know you did it of your own choice.'

He really just was such a great guy. Abbey felt like dirt. It wasn't a pleasant sensation. 'Thank you.'

'But when you do come back and we talk this through I think it only fair that I warn you I'll want a firmer commitment from you. I've waited a long time.' His eyes looked straight into hers. 'I don't think it's fair for you to expect me to wait any more.'

'So how did you meet Paul?'

Abbey turned her head to frown up at him as they walked along the pathway the next morning. 'We didn't come here to talk about Paul.'

Ethan shrugged his broad shoulders and looked ahead of them to the steep hill they were climbing. 'Just trying to get to know you, that's all. But if it's a touchy subject...'

'It's not a touchy subject. I just don't feel right talking to you about him, is all.'

'Fine.' He kept looking straight ahead. 'I'll try it another way, then. Do you feel the same way about him that you used to feel about me?'

Her breath caught in her chest at the question. 'You have no right to ask me that. It's none of your business.'

'Isn't it?' He glanced at her from the corner of his eye.

Abbey stopped and turned slightly to glare at him when he followed suit. 'We're here to talk about the past, aren't we? That's what this is all about. I fill in the gaps for you and then you leave. Paul has nothing to do with it.'

'I saw him drive away last night.'

She frowned. 'He had to go back to work.'

'He left you here with me.'

'I'm not *with* you. You're with Amy.'

Ethan thought again about correcting her on the untruth, but decided once again not to. It was easier somehow if she kept on believing he was as involved with someone else as she was. Defensive mode, he assumed. But, hey, it helped. Some.

She cocked her head to one side and quirked a dark brow at him. 'Is Amy happy with you being out here talking to me?'

'No.' He could answer that truthfully at least. Because he knew she wasn't. 'She's not.'

'Well, then.'

'And is he?'

Abbey gritted her teeth. 'Is he what?'

'Happy with you being out here talking to me?'

'What do you think?'

Ethan ignored the sharp edge to her tone. 'Then why'd he leave?'

Her temper got the better of her and she immediately snapped back with, 'Because I asked him to!'

And regretted the words the minute his eyes sparkled down at her. He saw Paul leaving as some kind of victory, didn't he? Damn him.

She watched with angry eyes as he turned and started back on the upward sloping path again. 'I don't think I'd have quit so quietly if I'd been him.'

'He didn't quit.' She spat the words at his back as she followed him. 'I asked him to give me some time and he had to go back to work anyway. We do actually happen to have a life when you're not around.'

Ethan smiled ahead. Somehow knowing that she'd been prepared to turn away the other guy so easily to spend time with him was quite gratifying.

Abbey had to lengthen her steps to get back in a position where she could see his face again. 'It's a life I'll be returning to very shortly too.'

He glanced sideways at her again. 'I have one of those too, you know. You don't have the monopoly on that.'

They continued walking in silence for a few moments as Abbey's temper gradually receded. In its place curiosity reared its head. 'What's it like?'

'What's what like?'

'Your life.' She stared ahead of her to the blue sky where it touched the brow of the hilltop they were walking towards. 'Where do you live now?'

'I live wherever the army sends me.'

'You're still in the army?'

'Yeah, I've got a few more years to go before I have to decide whether to stay in.'

'Did you get to fly?' He had talked about it over and over the summer they'd met. It had been his passion, the one thing he'd wanted more than he'd wanted her. At times she'd even been a little jealous, but when he talked about it his whole face had lit up and it had been hard to resist that enthusiasm.

He nodded and turned his head to grin at her. 'Oh, yeah. That part never loses its kick. I still get a buzz every time a chopper leaves the ground.'

She smiled back at him. 'You used to talk about it all the time. I knew more about helicopters by the end of the summer than I'd ever planned on knowing.'

'Hell, and you still wanted to talk to me?'

Her smile continued as she glanced away. 'You didn't exactly give me a big choice in that.'

'Persistent, was I?'

'That's one way of putting it.'

He laughed. 'That sounds like me.'

'The word *no* wasn't in your vocabulary.' She allowed the warmth of the memory to seep into her bones as the sun came out from behind a cloud and warmed her face.

The laughter continued. 'It still isn't.'

'Mmm.' She stole another peek at his profile. 'I noticed.'

Glancing across at her in the sunshine, he could understand why he'd have been so persistent with her. The light caught at strands of her hair and lit up her fair skin. She wasn't model material, but she was gorgeous nevertheless. Someone like her would have caught his attention straight away. Even if he hadn't had her photograph tucked in his wallet for years.

'How did we meet?'

'A kids' summer camp. Able-bodied and disabled kids. It was a voluntary programme for leaders from all round the world who were taking a break from college.'

'And we just hit it off?'

She laughed as she looked into his curious eyes. 'Hell, no. I thought you were an arrogant lump.'

Ethan's eyebrow raised at her as his eyes sparkled with amusement. 'I can see how we ended up married, then.'

'Well, like I said.' She glanced away from his sparkling eyes, her heart thumping a little harder. Obviously the exertion of climbing the steep hill. Nothing to do with the fact that that particular look reminded her of how he'd flirted with her those first few weeks. 'Like you said, you were persistent.'

'Wore you down, did I?'

She nodded a small nod. 'Something along those lines.'

He stopped walking again and turned to look at her. One large hand reached out to grasp hers and stop her in her tracks. 'You keep skirting over it all. *Tell me.*'

She tried to free her fingers from his hold with a turn of her hand. But he tightened his grasp and rubbed his thumb across the back of her smaller hand. Looking up, she frowned at him. 'What do you want me to tell you?'

'Everything.' The word came out soft and seductive. 'I want to know how you felt, what we talked about. Every detail. So that I can know it like you do.'

Swallowing to loosen the lump in her throat, she searched his face. 'I can't make it real to you. I can't put the pictures in your mind or the feelings into your heart. They're gone.'

'Not to you, though.'

No. Not to her. And that was why spending time with him was proving so difficult. Every time she looked into his face, as she was at that moment, she was remembering all that they'd been through together. Every word, every smile, every touch. And it was like re-opening a deep wound. Because it wasn't real any more. It was like some wonderful dream she'd had that she'd been haunted by night after night until eventually she'd been forced to let go of it.

'It's a part of my past.' She tried to ignore the warmth that was spreading up her arm from the caress of his thumb. 'I let go of it a long time ago.'

'You don't still feel it?'

'I feel pain when I remember it so I try not to remember.'

Ethan nodded in understanding. 'My being here probably doesn't help that, does it?'

'No.'

He tightened his fingers at the simple honesty of her answer. 'You'd prefer it if I'd never come to see you.'

Yes should have been her automatic response to his words, but somehow she knew it would be a lie. At least now she had the answer to why he'd never come to get her. Wondering why he hadn't would always have haunted her, no matter what she did with the rest of her life. She had to admit that it was better to have seen him than to have lived with a 'what if?' in the back of her mind.

'No. I guess it helps some to know you're okay. To know there was a reason.'

'You must have hated me.'

She nodded. 'Yes.'

His mouth twitched upwards at the corners. 'And called me a few names.'

Another nod. 'Oh, yes.'

His eyes grew serious as he asked the question that had been burning him since he'd got her letter. 'Why didn't you try to find out what had happened?'

'I wanted to.' She tried again to free herself from his hold. 'I believed for weeks that you'd call or write. You'd said it would take a while for you guys to drive back to Connecticut and that I shouldn't worry if it took a few days. So I waited.'

'And then?'

'Then I tried the cell number you gave me.'

Ethan shook his head. 'It got burned up in the car.'

'Burned?' Her eyes widened in shock at his words. She stopped trying to free her hand and squeezed his fingers instead. 'Burned, Ethan?'

He glanced down at their joined hands and nodded before looking back. 'The car caught fire just after we were pulled out. So they told me, anyway.'

Her heart twisted at the thought of him trapped inside that car when she'd been miles in the air above him. For the first time it hit

her that it could have been Ethan who died and
not Jamie. He could have died and she would
never have known. Because no one would
have known to tell her.

CHAPTER SEVEN

ETHAN'S eyes widened in stunned amazement as Abbey's eyes filled with tears.

'Hey.' He stepped closer with a frown on his face and freed her hand to gather her into his arms. 'What's wrong?'

Abbey swallowed a sob as her head rested against the warmth of his chest. She listened to the steady heartbeat against her ear while her own heart twisted into a painful knot in her chest.

'What is it?' He stroked her hair against her back and held her a little closer.

She shook her head against his chest and turned her face to hide it, breathing in the scent of him. She'd forgotten how great he smelled. Forgotten the familiarity of that scent. How could she have forgotten that?

He glanced down at the top of her head, tucked so neatly beneath his chin. What had he done wrong? Not five minutes ago she'd been standing arguing with him and now she was sobbing quietly against his chest. He frowned in confusion, keeping his voice as soothing as he knew how. 'What did I say?'

She sniffed and raised her head an inch from his chest. 'I'm sorry. I'm okay.'

He tightened his hold when she tried to pull away. Waited until she looked up at him with damp streaks on her cheeks. 'What?'

With a blink she tried to refocus. She cleared her throat with a small cough and looked down at the collar of his shirt. 'I guess I just hadn't thought about it.'

'About an accident you knew nothing about?' He frowned in confusion.

'No. About the fact that…' She cleared her throat again and aimed for some semblance of control. 'That you could have died and no one would ever have told me.'

'Hating me for never coming back might have been easier than knowing that.'

Her eyes flickered upwards to look into his.

Realization hit his mind. 'It's pretty much what did happen, though. You hated me for not coming back. You thought I was some bastard who had made promises he never meant to keep. The only difference was I wasn't dead. No one would have known to tell you either way.'

She continued to look at him, her eyes blinking as she followed his reasoning. 'But you were hurt and I didn't know. How hurt?'

He smiled a small smile. 'Pretty knocked about.'

'How much?' Her hands rose of their own accord to touch his sides where his shirt was tucked into his jeans.

With an upward glance he took a breath and then looked down at her face. 'Enough to keep me asleep for six weeks and in a hospital of some kind or another for four months.'

'You could have died too.'

He swallowed hard. 'I *should* have died too. Even the doctors thought that.'

Her fingers grabbed hold of his shirt and twisted it into her fists as she held onto him. 'I should have been there.'

'It wasn't your fault. Any more than it was my fault that I didn't know to come back for you.'

The tears welled again as she nodded up at him. He was right. There wasn't anything that either of them could have done to have changed things. They had happened and that was that. That was what life had thrown their way. And somehow knowing that helped her to let go of the anger she'd felt at him for breaking her heart. It was ironic. In supposedly helping Ethan to fill in the gaps that he felt from those missing months when they'd met, she'd actually given herself a form of the closure she'd been looking for.

'I know.'

Ethan looked down into her eyes and saw the small smile that moved across her mouth. His heart caught in a way he couldn't remember it ever having caught before.

Without reasoning out whether or not it was the appropriate thing to do he pulled her back against his chest. Simply because it felt like the right thing to do.

'Does this mean you forgive me?'

She smiled against his chest. 'I guess it does.'

'Then my being here helped in a way.'

She nodded. 'I guess it did.'

'Was I this helpful before?'

She laughed. 'Oh, yeah, all the time. Every time I yapped, you helped out straight away.'

He tightened his hold for a brief second. 'I'm glad.'

She allowed herself a few extra minutes' comfort in being against his body and held so close. But then, with a breath, she found the strength to pull back from him and let go. Straightening her clothes with the flat of her hands, she glanced up at him from beneath long lashes. 'Talking to you wasn't supposed to be therapeutic for *me*.'

'That's all right. It's helping me some too.' He glanced at her with a half-smile, then looked up the hill. 'So we still walking up this hill or what?'

She glanced in the same direction. 'It's worth it when you get to the top.'

'Go on then, Irish girl.' He swept his arm in a wide arc in the direction of the path. 'You lead the way.'

Glad to be given something safer to do, she took another breath and started walking again.

Silence drifted over them bar the song of birds in the trees that surrounded either side of their path. Abbey felt a sense of calmness wash over her that she hadn't felt in a long time. It was weird, but it was also a feeling she'd missed. Having such control over every other aspect of her life had obviously not been as fulfilling as she'd thought it would be. But she was also aware of the fact that she couldn't rely on Ethan's presence to make things better either. After all, this was just a stop-off of sorts. A few fleeting hours where they could put things to rest. That was all. She frowned slightly.

'What's the frown for?'

She shook her head. 'You don't miss a damn thing, do you?'

'It's a useful character trait when you're flying a chopper. Occupational hazard.'

'I'd imagine so.'

Ethan allowed himself the odd look in her direction as they walked. He felt uncomfortable, awkward almost. Not surprising really. It wasn't as if he went around hugging strangers every day of his life. His eyes glanced down at her hand where it swung next to her body as she walked. He frowned as he felt the sudden urge to reach out for that hand again and hold it as they walked. What was he all of a sudden—an Abbey addict?

'It's obviously contagious, whatever it is.'

He looked up at her and grinned when her meaning sunk in. 'Not a walk in the park, this therapy thing.'

She laughed at his choice of words, considering where they were walking. 'No, it's not. Maybe we should pick something to talk about rather than winging it.'

'That might help.'

They continued walking, the brow of the hill getting closer with every step. Then as Ethan looked up the landscape opened before him like a picture from a postcard. He doubted he'd have got a better view from the cockpit of a chopper.

'Wow. That's something else.'

Abbey smiled as she watched his face, then allowed her eyes to follow the same direction as his over the rolling hills in varying shades of green.

'It's not called the Emerald Isle for nothing.'

It took his breath away. As far as the eye could see there were fields and forests. With a turn of his head he smiled across at her. 'I can understand why you live here.'

Her dark eyes continued looking out over the panorama she never grew tired of seeing and she smiled a soft smile as she remembered. 'We used to look out over the lake at night at the camp and talk about this place. It was the first place you wanted to see when you came here.'

He turned his head and looked at her face as she continued looking forward.

'We were going to travel around Ireland and see everywhere before I went back with you.' Her breasts rose and fell as she took a deep breath of the clear, crisp air. 'You used to do this dumb impersonation of an Irish accent in preparation for the trip. It was really awful.'

A smile spread across his face. 'Sorry.'

Her eyes sparkled across at him. 'It's okay. It was cute.'

He grimaced. 'God, now I really am sorry.'

Abbey laughed.

Ethan was caught off guard by the warm sound. She had a great laugh, warm and lilting. He could understand why he'd have done dumb things to get her to do it. His mind turned over, his eyes sparkled and he asked, 'What else did we get up to by that lake, then?'

Her smile faded and a flush spread over her cheeks as she looked away from him. 'The stuff that two people do by a lake at night, I guess.'

'I'd like to hear about that stuff. And that time at the beach too.' He hadn't forgotten how embarrassed she'd been when they'd made cocktails.

'I'll let you use your imagination on those things.'

'Oh, you don't know how active my imagination can be.'

'Actually, yes, I do.' The flush grew in strength. She turned from the view and looked back down the path. 'We should go back now.'

Ethan stepped in front of her and looked down until her eyes eventually lifted to meet his. 'Maybe you should show me.'

'What?' Her eyes widened in surprise.

He shrugged. 'When you talk about our past your face lights up. The memories mean something to you even now, don't they?'

Her breath caught.

'You say they're in the past, but they're not really. They're as real to you as if they happened yesterday.'

She continued staring even as she admitted inwardly that he was right.

'I'll be gone in a few days.'

Her heart caught at the words. It was what she wanted him to do, but hearing it didn't come any easier.

'And when I go I want to understand what it felt like to love someone enough to run off and get married. Because I've never felt that since then. I'm not a ''run off and get married'' kind of guy.'

Her eyebrow quirked slightly. It wasn't entirely true. But she didn't open her mouth to correct him.

His eyes burned into hers as he took a small step closer. 'I don't think that talking about the past will help me remember any better. They're your memories now. Not mine.'

'Then why are we here?'

Maybe it had been the moment when he'd held her while she'd cried. Maybe it had been listening to some of the things she remembered. Whatever it was, suddenly he needed more. Ethan surprised himself by speaking the words aloud only seconds after he'd realized the truth of it himself: 'I need to know the woman in the photo. You.'

'What will that achieve? You just said you can't get the memories back, so what good is it going to do knowing me now?'

He stopped when his body was inches from hers, encouraged by the fact that she hadn't moved away. 'Because then I'll understand why we got married.'

'What exactly are you suggesting we do for you to understand that?'

Without speaking he reached out and cupped her face with his hands. He looked into her startled eyes for a split second and then lowered his mouth to hers.

As Abbey gasped he stole the sound from her mouth. This couldn't be happening again! She moaned, almost in anguish, as he moved his warm mouth over hers and shifted his body closer. This wasn't supposed to be happening. All they were supposed to do was talk. Just words. Not kissing. Not touching!

His hands moved along the sides of her face, across her smooth skin, into her hair as he turned his head slightly to deepen the kiss.

She was drowning again. How could he still do this to her? How could he make her feel as if the world had just tilted underneath her feet? How could he make her head spin that way? It wasn't fair!

She struggled back from his hold, dragged her lips from his and moved her hands up to tug his from her face.

'You can't keep doing this, Ethan!'

He stared down at her with hooded eyes. 'Can't I?'

'No, you can't!' She brought her hands to her warm cheeks, moved to smooth her hair back into place. 'We're not together any more. I'm with someone else; you're with someone else—'

He opened his mouth to tell her the truth only to be interrupted as she continued, 'If you think I'm going to jump into bed with you every day for the next few days so you can put some ghosts to rest, then you're sorely mistaken.'

'That's not damn well what I'm suggesting we do!'

'Then what *is* this?' She stared at him with confusion on her face. 'What are you trying to do?'

He stared down at her in anger. Anger because the truth was he wasn't entirely sure. He

just knew that he wanted to kiss her again.
Maybe it was some deeply hidden memory
that drew him to it, but if it was deeply hidden
then how could he possibly know that was the
reason? All he knew was he was attracted to
her. Was drawn to her. And the only way he
knew of to find out what that meant was to
actually follow the impulse through.

'Are you telling me you don't feel anything
when you're with me?'

Her jaw dropped.

'Because if you can tell me that you're completely over this thing we had, then I'll leave
you be.'

Breathing was rapidly becoming a very difficult function as she continued to gape at him.

He stepped forward again and frowned
when she immediately jumped back from him.
'But I don't think you are. If you were, you'd
have just sorted a divorce from here instead of
writing to me. You *wanted* to see me, A.J. You
wanted to know what happened. And now you
know. And you know it wasn't my fault. So

now I want to see if what we had eight years ago is still there.'

She shook her head as she continued to back away. He couldn't be saying these things. Not even ten minutes ago she'd realized she was actually getting some closure on a part of her life that had hurt so much. And now he was trying, not only to take that from her, but to make her live through it all again. She couldn't do it. She damn well *wouldn't* do it!

'It's not. It's gone.' She flung the words at him. 'You have a new life, I have a new life and they couldn't be any further apart.'

'And what if we're meant to be together?'

'If we were meant to be together, then we would have been before now!'

Ethan studied her face for a long moment and stated what was immediately obvious to him. 'You're scared.'

Damn right she was scared. Scared of finding out that he couldn't love her again, scared of having her heart broken all over again, scared of giving everything up on the slimmest of chances that there was still such a thing left as a great romance.

'I can understand that.'

'How the hell can you possibly understand that? You don't know me!'

'I want to know you!'

They stood a few feet from each other and glared, anger surrounding them. Abbey shook her head as she studied his face. 'You have to let this go, Ethan.'

'Like you have?' He smiled sarcastically.

'Yes, like I have!' She shouted the lie at him. 'Because I had no choice. I lost the man I loved the day that truck hit you as surely as I would have done if you'd died.'

'But I didn't die!'

The tears pooled in her eyes again as she stepped further away, her voice dropping. 'The part of you that loved me did. And I can't bring that back.'

His voice softened. 'You could try.'

'No. I can't.' She shook her head again. 'It's too bloody late.'

CHAPTER EIGHT

MAYBE he should have gone after her.

Ethan thought about it an hour or two later on the walk down from the hill towards the village. Maybe he should have, but he hadn't. He hadn't because it had hurt too much to try and risk another rejection. And he didn't know why that was.

After all, the simple fact was that he had met Abbey for the 'first time' less than three days ago. He shouldn't have felt as if he'd just been kicked in the teeth. He shouldn't have suddenly realized how damned lonely he was.

If he didn't remember a thing about their time together before, then why did it feel as if he lost something every time she walked away?

He went over and over the conversation they'd had, the small snippets of information she'd given him about their time together.

She'd mentioned how determined he'd been back then. *Persistent,* as he had said. It was exactly the way he'd always been in the things he wanted. And he could understand completely having wanted her then. Because he wanted her now.

But why?

Ethan considered his life to be pretty well balanced. He enjoyed his job—hell, he'd wanted to fly helicopters since he'd been old enough to pronounce the word properly. And despite the set-back caused by the accident he'd still managed to complete the training.

He had a great family. His parents still married after forty years and still disgustingly happy.

A great bunch of friends both in and out of the service, even though he still felt the gap left by Jamie. And it wasn't as if he hadn't had girlfriends along the way.

So why did he feel so strong a pull towards Abbey?

Maybe just by looking at the photograph for all these years he had convinced himself that she was familiar, that he knew her. Even if he didn't remember her. It would be some kind of an explanation. A pretty lame one, but an explanation nevertheless.

So what now?

He stopped at a gateway and looked back up the hill they'd been standing on.

She still had to have some feelings for him. She could deny it all she wanted, fight with him about it and keep on running away. But he knew there still had to be something there for her to fight against it so hard.

Knowing that fact certainly gave him the incentive to fight further himself. To continue being *persistent*. But it didn't necessarily give him a right...

Because what was it he expected from her, after all? A short-lived affair to get her ghost out of his system so he could move on, as she had? Or maybe something a little more long-term? Like, maybe staying married...

It was one hell of a step.

The fact was he didn't want to think that far ahead. He just wanted to know what it all meant. Why *did* he feel so drawn to her? Was their relationship that once-in-a-lifetime thing that his parents had? If it was he would be a fool to walk away from it. Or to allow her to walk away from it either.

But if she kept on pushing him away how was he supposed to get to know her better? He needed to get to know her in order to get close.

He thought about the problem for a while. All women confided in their mothers, right? So he'd go make friends with her mom...

'I can stay, you know.'

'I know.' Abbey smiled encouragingly at Karyn as she continued to fold things away into her weekend case. The case's contents could have supplied her with a new outfit every day for a month if she mixed and matched, so clothing wouldn't have been a problem. 'But, really, I'm not going to be that far behind you.'

Karyn held a pair of folded trousers against her chest as she studied her friend's face. 'The chat with Ethan didn't go well, I'm guessing.'

'That would be one interpretation of how it went.'

'What happened?'

'He kissed me again.'

Karyn's eyes rounded dramatically. 'Really?'

Abbey nodded ruefully. 'Uh-huh.'

Throwing the neatly folded trousers into a heap on top of her case, she sat down on the end of the bed and waved her hand towards her breasts. 'Give with the details, honey.'

Abbey smiled at Karyn's enthusiasm for gossip. 'It's not funny.'

'Who said it was?'

'And I don't want an ''I told you so'' either.'

'Cross my heart.' She crossed it with one long red fingernail.

'He still doesn't remember anything about before but he seems to have this idea that if we just ''got to know each other better'' it might be a good idea.'

'Define ''get to know each other better''.'

Abbey raised her eyebrows.

'Ah, that ''get to know each other better'','
Karyn nodded wisely. 'I see.'

'Good, then you can explain it to me, 'cos
I just don't get it.'

'I told you I thought he had the hots for
you.'

'He doesn't *know* me.'

'But he wants to. That has to mean something, doesn't it? And it has to be hard to resist
if you still have feelings for him.'

'I don't!'

It was Karyn's turn to raise her eyebrows.

Abbey groaned and placed her palms over
her face. 'Okay, maybe I do, but not for him
the way he is now.' She peeked out from behind her hands. 'I have feelings for the person
I married and he's gone.'

'No, he's not. He's right here in Killyduff
in all his six-foot glory.'

'But he's not the same guy.' She pleaded
her case. 'The guy I loved loved me back. The
feelings were mutual and we had a foundation,
a beginning with shared memories. We don't
have that any more. We've both moved on.'

'Have you? You've still not given Paul a yes-or-no answer.' She held her hand up in front of her when Abbey's mouth opened. 'And you can't fob me off with that whole "needing to let go of Ethan before you said yes to Paul" crap, because, now I've seen Ethan, I think we both know that Paul isn't the one for you.'

'Paul's—'

'Yeah, yeah, you've said, a great guy. I got it.'

'I was going to say, ideal for my life.'

'That's romantic.'

Abbey dropped backwards onto the bed and stared at the ceiling. 'It's sensible, is what it is. Romance doesn't last. Paul and I have a relationship that's built on mutual respect and understanding. It's practical. That's a much more lasting thing than romance.'

'And boring as hell. You may as well marry an electric kettle if that's the depth of your emotions.'

She turned her head to frown up at her friend. 'Why shouldn't I settle for someone as suitable as Paul? I like him, he's a—'

Karyn smiled.

'Well, he damn well is!'

'But he doesn't flick your switches, honey, and Ethan does. And there's a lot to be said for that.'

'So you think I should just quit my job and move halfway across the world to be an army wife?'

'He's in the army?'

'Chopper pilot.'

Karyn grinned. *'Yum.'*

'Stop it.'

'Sorry.' She lay down on the bed beside Abbey and propped an elbow to rest her head. 'You could have a career anywhere you want. Good promotions agencies exist all over the world. And you have to have thought about all that before.'

'I did. When I was twenty-two and hadn't built myself a life. I have more to lose now.' She turned on her side and propped her elbow in the same manner as Karyn's. 'And it's not like he was suggesting we stay married and live happily ever after. He has a *girlfriend* with him.'

'You're kidding.'

'Nope, my height, blonde, pretty as hell.'

'You met her?' Karyn gaped at her.

'She was leaving Ethan's room when I went to see him last night.'

'Sister?'

'He doesn't have a sister and anyway…' she frowned down at the duvet cover '…Ethan was half naked when she was leaving the room.'

Karyn mulled over her words for a moment. 'The plot thickens. Why would he bring a girl-friend with him to meet his wife?'

'Beats the hell out of me. But you gotta admit, from her point of view, if your boyfriend got a letter from someone claiming to be his wife, wouldn't you want to keep tabs on him while he went for a wee visit?'

The red fingernail waggled in the air between them. 'You've got a point there.'

They both turned and lay on their backs to stare at the ceiling.

'He still made a pass at you even though he has a girlfriend.'

'Yep. That sucks, doesn't it?'

'Maybe she's just ideal for the life he has now.'

'Ha, ha.'

Karyn recognized the sarcasm in Abbey's voice. 'Was he the kind of guy who would keep two women on the go when you met him?'

'No.'

'Then maybe he's not any happier in his relationship than you are in yours.'

Abbey turned her head on the duvet to frown. 'I *am* happy.'

Karyn looked round with a raised eyebrow.

Abbey frowned harder. 'Well, I'm content.'

Karyn smirked.

'Aw, hell.' She turned her head back to look at the ceiling. 'Now I'm breaking up with Paul too?'

'Surely you're curious as to why Ethan would be prepared to bring a girlfriend all the way over here to cheat on her?'

She closed her eyes as the question echoed in her brain. It wasn't like Ethan to cheat on someone. It just wasn't in him. Or at least it hadn't been when she'd known him. He'd have seen it as dishonourable in a way. Disloyal at the very least. When she'd known him he'd been honest and faithful. She'd never felt a need to distrust him, even when half the female camp leaders had thrown themselves in front of him.

'He wouldn't do that.'

'You said you didn't know him any more.'

'I don't believe he'd have changed that much.'

Karyn thought for another moment. 'Maybe she's not his girlfriend.'

Abbey shook her head. 'He'd have said so.'

They lay in silence for several more silent minutes, then Karyn's voice broke the silence again. 'Well, I'm sure as hell not leaving now.'

Eyes still closed, Abbey smiled towards the ceiling. 'Thanks.'

'Sweetie, I'm not just staying for you. This is way too good to miss.'

CHAPTER NINE

THE woman's face registered surprise when she opened the door to him. 'I can't imagine what you think you're doing here, young man.'

Ethan smiled what he hoped was a charming smile. 'Actually, I came to talk to you.'

'Abigail isn't married to you.'

Abigail? He smiled all the more at the name. 'Abigail may not be, but Abbey is.'

'I think I would know if my daughter was married.'

'She didn't tell you.'

'There is no way on earth I would ever have allowed my daughter to marry some American I've never met before.' She raised her chin an inch as she stared at him with eyes a paler brown than Abbey's.

'Maybe that's why she didn't tell you.'

She seemed to consider his words for a moment before her shoulders slumped a barely perceptible inch. 'She'd have told her father.'

Ethan raised an eyebrow. 'And wouldn't he have told you?'

'My husband died several years ago.'

He hadn't known that. But how could he? 'Were they close?'

'Abigail and her father?'

He nodded.

'Yes, inseparable. She took the loss rather hard.'

'I'm sure you both did, Mrs Jackman.'

She seemed to soften slightly at his words, her eyes studying his face intently. 'If you're my daughter's husband, then where, may I ask, have you been for all this time?'

'That's a long story.'

Again she studied him with her piercing gaze and then nodded, as if some major decision had been made. 'Well, if Abigail won't talk to me, then I'll have to listen to what you have to say, won't I?'

He smiled again. 'I'd appreciate that.'

'You'd best come in.' She turned away from the large door and moved down the hallway. 'I'm assuming that you Americans drink tea?'

'If it's chilled, ma'am.'

She tutted as she continued walking. 'Only across the water…'

'So what was the kiss like?'

Abbey opened her eyes to stare at the ceiling again. 'It was like every kiss I ever remember having with Ethan.'

'Hot, huh?'

She smiled and turned her head. 'Yes.' Then she frowned. 'But I can't go through another involvement with him, Karyn.'

'Still hurts, does it?'

'Yes.' She'd spent years not talking about her feelings for Ethan and now it actually felt good to have someone listen. Sometimes a problem carried alone became heavier for the fact it was *being* carried alone. 'Being with him brings it all back. I even cried all over him today.'

'Because he kissed you?'

The words didn't raise a smile. 'No, before that. We were talking about the accident and it hit me that if he'd died I'd never have known.'

'God.' Karyn propped herself up on her elbow again. 'No one would have known you had to know, would they?'

'Not with Jamie gone. He was the only other person who knew. Well…' she raised her brows slightly at the memory '…Jamie and some random soul we talked into being the other witness.'

'You could have spent years hating his guts and he could have been dead all that time. Makes you think.'

They heard the doorbell ring in the distance.

Abbey lifted her head to look at the closed door. 'Mother will get it.'

'You still haven't talked to her, have you?'

'No, that one I can wait for.'

'I'll bet.'

She lay back down again. 'It just really hurt to think that he was hurt, could have died, while over here I was already breaking my heart over him.'

'It's dramatic stuff, all right. But at least now you know it wasn't a case of he didn't come get you because he didn't love you.'

'Actually, I now know exactly that in a roundabout way.'

'That's not his doing, though. It wasn't his choice.'

She sighed. 'I know. But it doesn't make it any better.'

They heard the rumble of voices in the distance as people walked down the hallway below their room. Karyn studied Abbey's profile. 'So you're just gonna let him go, are you?'

'Who are we talking about now?'

She smiled. 'Ethan.'

'I have to. What else can I do?'

'You could take a chance.'

'I could get hurt all over again.'

Karyn nodded. 'Yes, you could. But that's the game we all play. Big risks for big gains, honey. You've already had something so great once with this man that you made a huge commitment to him. One that, knowing you, you didn't take lightly.'

She raised her head again to stare at Karyn. 'I meant the words, you know. Till death do us part.'

'Then if you meant those vows you have to take another chance.'

'Even if he has a new girlfriend?'

Karyn shrugged. 'We could bump her off. It's a small town, millions of miles from any-where. It would take years to find a body.'

'I think my husband would notice she'd gone.' She smiled despite her best efforts not to.

Karyn's face was deadpan. A lesser friend might even have taken her seriously. 'Well, hon, you'd just have to keep him distracted, then.'

They sat down to tea, the hot variety, in a large conservatory at the back of the house. Ethan looked out over the perfect lawn and tended beds. 'You have a lovely home here.'

'I like to take a pride in it.' Abbey's mother raised her chin again as she looked at the gar-den, then surprised him by turning her head and smiling. 'But it's getting a little much now without the children here.'

'You're thinking of moving?'

'I think it's time.'

'It'll be tough letting go of it, though, I'll bet.' He sipped at the warm liquid and found it wasn't actually all that bad.

'Letting go of something that means a lot to a person is sometimes necessary. So that that person can move forward with their life.'

A dark eyebrow quirked slightly at her choice of words. She wasn't actually talking about the house now, was she? He glanced up from the edge of his cup and smiled a small smile at her open study of him. 'Sometimes a person has to understand the past before they can decide what to do with their future.'

'Is that why you came here?'

'In a roundabout way. I didn't know I was married.'

His statement surprised her, her cup halting its upwards progress in mid-air. 'How could you not know that? I'm assuming you had to

be present at the ceremony. Or are things really
that different where you come from?'

'They're not that different, ma'am. I was in
an accident and I have...' he tilted his head
'...a few gaps.'

'But you must remember my daughter in order to be here.'

'No. She wrote me a letter to check we were
divorced and that's how I found out.'

Elizabeth sipped her tea as she considered
his words. 'So you're here to see about a divorce, then.'

Ethan took a breath and opened up to yet
another stranger. 'No, actually, I think I want
to find out why we got married in the first
place.'

'You think you still have feelings for her?'

'I don't know.' He shrugged, a warmth
spreading over his skin at the older woman's
scrutiny. 'And Abbey isn't too keen to let me
close enough to find out.'

Elizabeth nodded. 'Abigail is very good at
closing the door in people's faces.'

'That's kinda why I thought you might
help me.'

*   *   *

'Distraction is something that might just backfire on me.'

'Oh, damn, he's that good?'

Abbey blushed a deep crimson and turned her head again to look at Karyn's sparkling eyes. 'Some people just have chemistry and we had it. By the bucketload.'

'I'll bet you don't have *that* with Paul.'

'Well, Paul has this…theory.'

'Do tell.' Her eyes widened.

'He's been burned a few times, you see…'

'Haven't we all, hon?'

'Yes, but he decided to try and build something more lasting by trying some old-fashioned values.'

Karyn wriggled a little closer, her voice dropping. *'Like?'*

'Like no sex before marriage.'

Her friend's eyes widened to the size of dinner plates. After several seconds of silence where she stared with her jaw dropped, she eventually grinned and replied with, 'Any bloody wonder he wants to get married!'

Abbey turned her head back to the ceiling, sighed and then sat up. 'I knew you wouldn't get this.'

'Aw, c'mon, Abbey, no sex at all? Nothing? And you're still with him while you have Mr Sex-on-legs as a husband? And you have to *think* about this?'

She glared sideways at Karyn. 'There's more to a marriage than just sex!'

'I'm sure there is, but it's a big part to just ignore when you're even *considering* getting married. You know we had a recent change or two of century there, don't you?'

'I'd heard.' She stood up and turned around to look down at Karyn's prone figure. 'But, actually, I happened to think it was sweet, and at least it showed he wasn't just interested in me for just the one thing.'

As Karyn pushed herself into a sitting position she studied Abbey's face and then a light bulb seemed to go on somewhere. 'Oh, no, I get it. It worked for you because then you didn't have to make a commitment.'

'We've been dating for months!'

'Like he was some sort of bosom buddy, not like a serious, involved relationship with a member of the opposite sex.'

Abbey threw her arms up in exasperation. 'Fine, whatever you want to think.'

'Because you can't get involved with Paul like that when you still love Ethan, can you, honey?'

'I don't know how I can help you.'

Ethan set down his cup and leaned a little closer. 'You could start by telling me if she's really in love with this Paul guy.'

'I can tell you I would really quite like it if she were in love with ''this Paul guy'', as you call him. He's highly suitable for her. And at least it would show she's capable of making a commitment to *someone*.'

Ethan smiled. 'She kinda already did.'

Elizabeth pondered his words again, a small frown appearing on her forehead. 'That's the thing I find the hardest to believe. If my daughter was in love enough to marry you, then she'd have found it nigh on impossible to let go of you. She's like her father that way.'

'A mate for life kinda thing?' His smile grew at the thought. Wasn't that what everyone looked for deep down? The thought that she'd have felt that way about him made him happy for some reason.

'Yes.' Her words came slowly. 'I believe that's exactly what I meant.'

His voice dropped as he leaned a little closer. 'Then I might just have a chance here?'

Elizabeth seemed to warm to his air of hopefulness. 'I believe you might at that.'

One large hand reached forward to reach for hers. 'It's good to hear that. I'm glad I came to talk to you.'

'You're never going to quit on this, are you?'

'Not while you continue being such an idiot about it, no.'

Abbey sighed and shook her head. 'What do you want me to say, Karyn? I'm still in love

with Ethan, I've never in my life loved someone like I loved Ethan, and I'll probably never
completely get over Ethan?'

'You could just say yes, because all of those
things are true.'

Abbey's eyelashes dropped down to brush
her cheeks as she frowned hard and fought
against the knot in her chest. Since the moment
she'd made the decision to write her damned
letter she'd been fighting a battle and the fight
had got harder since Ethan had come back and
the world had found out about him. What was
the point in fighting in this one tiny room with
only Karyn to bear witness?

'Yes.'

Karyn waited until she looked back at her
with tormented eyes. Then she grinned widely.
'I know.'

Abbey smiled back for the briefest instant.
'But that doesn't mean there's a happily ever
after here. Because there isn't.'

'Why isn't there?' She seemed puzzled by
the very idea.

'Because life just doesn't work out like
that.'

CHAPTER TEN

ETHAN talking to her mother was the very last thing she expected to see when they eventually came down to make tea.

She heard their voices filter through from the conservatory and her eyes widened as she looked at Karyn.

'No way,' she whispered across at her friend.

Karyn grinned as they both moved across the kitchen to stand in the doorway to the conservatory.

Ethan glanced up and smiled as she approached. 'Hi.'

Hi?

'What the hell do you think you're doing?'

'Abigail!' Her mother's expression was one of outrage. 'Really, there's no need to be so rude.'

'Stay out of this, Mother.' She glared over at her. 'Just for once in your life.'

As Ethan looked at Elizabeth he saw her straighten her back and a cool expression fix onto her face. He frowned at Abbey. 'Don't take it out on your mom. My being here wasn't her idea.'

Elizabeth smiled as she leaned forward to pat Ethan's knee. 'That's quite all right. Abigail vents her frustrations on me regularly.'

'I do not!'

Her mother blinked up at her.

Abbey subdued her temper in an almost teenage-like manner. 'No more than you vent yours on me.'

'Mother-daughter relationships are often difficult.'

Elizabeth's words caught her off guard and interrupted her train of thought. 'Since when did you become so understanding?'

'Maybe since someone involved in your life actually took the time to talk to me.'

'I talk to you.'

Elizabeth blinked again, a small smile on her mouth. 'Not in several years, you haven't. I think we're both well aware of that fact.'

Abbey blinked back at her and looked at Karyn for help when words failed her. Karyn merely shrugged back at her.

'Don't look at me.'

She looked back at her mother, then pointed a finger at Ethan. '*He* shouldn't be here.'

'When you won't talk to the people who care about you, it's only natural that they end up talking to each other.'

It was surreal. She shook her head to bring the world into focus. 'Mother, you like *Paul*. So why are you talking to Ethan?'

'Isn't it natural for a mother to want to get to know the man her daughter is married to?'

'There's no point in you trying to get to know him when he has nothing to do with my life any more!'

'I think he does.'

'I kinda think I do.'

Abbey glared as they smiled at each other, having spoken simultaneously. 'He does not!

And pretty soon he'll be gone so unless you're planning on being penfriends there is absolutely no point in this.'

'And what if I decide I'm not going away?'

Her attention was drawn back to Ethan as he spoke the determined words. 'What the hell do you mean you're not going away? I'd have thought the army might have something to say about you not going back...'

Ethan held his ground and looked at her with a calm expression. 'I may go back, but that doesn't mean I won't come back here again.'

'You can't do that.'

'You can't stop me.'

She looked again to Karyn for some help, but her frustration grew when she smiled in an 'I told you so' kind of a way.

With a tilt of her head she looked him in the eye. 'And what exactly would you achieve by being my own personal stalker?'

Ethan shrugged. 'I might eventually break down those barriers of yours enough for you to let me get to know you again.'

'You do make it difficult for people to get close to you, dear.' Her mother supported Ethan with her words. 'You obviously cared about this person enough to marry him and I doubt, knowing what little I do of your life, that that happens very often.'

'I think you'd best not pick holes in my perfect world 'til we've had a closer look at yours, don't you?'

Ethan's eyes moved to Karyn and she grimaced. She knew all about the difficulties of Abbey's relationship with her mother, but it couldn't have been easy for Ethan to understand.

'I know I've made mistakes, but that doesn't mean I want you to do the same thing.'

'So I should just drop everything and run off with someone who doesn't even know how I take a cup of coffee?'

'Or your eggs in the morning.' His eyes sparkled. 'But that doesn't mean I wouldn't be interested in finding out.'

Her eyes shot across to meet his, her face flushing. 'Wouldn't it be a bit crowded at breakfast with your *girlfriend* there?'

Elizabeth stared at Ethan's profile. 'You have a girlfriend?'

He turned to look at her, his expression rueful. 'No, ma'am, I don't.'

'Yes, you bloody do.'

His eyes went back to hers. 'Actually, no, I *bloody* don't.'

His calmness made her anger rise again. It came out as sarcasm. 'So that woman who left your hotel room while you were naked was just a good friend, was she?'

'Yes.' He looked back at Elizabeth. 'And technically I wasn't naked. I had a towel on.'

Only just, if Abbey's memory served, but that was beside the point. 'So your good friend always shares a bed with you, does she?'

'She hasn't shared a bed with me since she was four and she has her own room at the hotel.'

'Ah.'

Abbey turned her attention to Karyn as she spoke the word, her eyebrows raising interrogatively. *'Ah?'*

'Ah, as in "Ah, that makes more sense, doesn't it?"'

It didn't. Well, not in Abbey's mind it didn't. 'She just traipsed halfway round the world to show you some moral support?'

He smiled affectionately. 'She's seen herself as some kind of bodyguard since the accident. It was Amy who stood by me while I went through all the rehab.'

Abbey's heart twisted in her chest. The unknown woman had been there for him. It had been Amy who had been there to help him through instead of her. *She'd* been the one to support him, to care enough that he made it through.

When it should have been Abbey herself.

Unreasonably, it made her dislike the woman all the more.

'You let me think she was your girlfriend.' She folded her arms across her aching heart and raised her chin in defence.

'You assumed she was, and we were arguing a lot at the time, so I didn't correct you.'

'The fact that you know Abbey has a boy-friend probably didn't help any.'

Abbey stared again at her mother. Did the woman's empathy with Ethan know no bounds? She'd known her mother her whole life and never known her to take to someone so quickly.

'Well, the term ''boyfriend'' might be a stretch.'

She closed her eyes at Karyn's addition to the conversation. Opening them slowly, she rewarded her with a warning glare before looking back into Ethan's questioning eyes. 'You still could have told me.'

'Rather than find out you were jealous, you mean?'

She wanted to scream in frustration. 'Why can't you just go away, Ethan?'

He blinked up at her with his warm hazel eyes and smiled softly as he spoke the words. 'There must be something holding me back, I guess.'

Every female bar Abbey smiled back at him and Abbey was vaguely surprised that neither of them went 'Aw' at him. If she'd been less in control she might even have said the word herself.

'Well, it's not me. You could leave any time.'

'And you wouldn't miss me?'

Her traitorous heart twisted again beneath her arms and truthful words escaped under a veil of sarcasm. 'I'd learn to live with it.'

'Give him a chance, Abigail.' Elizabeth's words were soft. 'Would that be so very hard for you to do?'

'Why are you on his team all of a sudden? You don't even know him.' The open wound that Ethan had created seemed to seep into other wounds of old. 'Or is it just that you'll do anything to keep having some control over my life?'

Elizabeth's calm features transformed with surprise. 'I don't try to control your life.'

'Mother, you've always tried to control my life. You didn't even want me to go to America in the first place. It was Dad who talked you round.'

There was a pause before sadness crossed her eyes and she sighed. 'Because I didn't want to let you go.'

'You wanted to control my life.'

'No, I didn't want to lose you. You were already growing away from us, from home, and I thought if you stretched your wings that far you might never come back.' She looked down to where she'd folded her hands gracefully in her lap. 'And I wasn't ready to let go of my youngest child.'

Abbey stared in shock as the simple honesty of the words sank in. Somehow it had never occurred to her that the control her mother had tried to exert over her wasn't because she was trying to interfere, but merely because she was afraid. When her brothers had left, she should have known that. So why had she been so blind?

'You never said that.'

Her mother's smile was weary when she looked up. 'I spoke to your father about it and he persuaded me that in order to have you come back to us, I had to let you go. I always hoped he was right about that. He was always so right about everything else.'

Suddenly she could hear all the things her father had said about her mother's need to hold onto things. He'd always been quick to defend her when Abbey had griped as a teenager, and at the time Abbey had honestly believed it was because he'd just wanted to keep the peace. After all, there had been times when he'd escaped from Elizabeth along with her.

But maybe he'd just occasionally wanted time to himself. Maybe he'd just wanted time with his only daughter. Maybe the strong, quiet man she'd loved so dearly had actually loved his wife more than he'd told his children. Because he'd understood her more than they ever could have. That was what years of being together meant, wasn't it?

Not for the first time in the last few days, Abbey felt tears pool in her eyes. She swallowed hard as she looked at her mother. 'You couldn't even hug me when he died.'

Silent tears appeared in Elizabeth's eyes. 'Because you wouldn't come near me long enough for me to try.'

'I was alone, Mother.'

'So was I, Abbey.'

'He loved you.' She voiced the thought she suddenly knew with a greater clarity than she'd ever known before. When he'd been alive she'd never thought of it as being a once-in-a-lifetime kind of love. She'd thought it was just the way they were. They'd been together half their lives. It had been habit, if nothing else. But in her heart she now knew. She just knew. 'He really loved you.'

Elizabeth's smile was the most open Abbey could ever remember seeing. 'Not as much as he loved you. I could never compete with you from the moment you were born. He said it was because you reminded him so much of me.' She laughed ruefully. 'But somehow I doubt you'd have enjoyed hearing that.'

Abbey laughed the same laugh along with her. 'I'd have hated it.'

One hand rose from her lap to wipe at the dampness beneath her eyes as Elizabeth turned to smile at Ethan. 'My husband was a wonderful man, Ethan. I think you'd have liked

him. Though he'd have given you quite a grilling before he'd ever have allowed you to be
with his little girl.'

'I'd have respected that. I hope I'll be the
same way with my daughter some day.' Ethan
glanced at Abbey as he spoke, then smiled
back at her mother. 'I'm sorry I didn't get to
meet him.'

'It was a very long illness. Cancer.' She
frowned as a realization came to her and she
looked up at her daughter. 'It wasn't that very
long after you came back from America that
we all found out. You must have needed Ethan
desperately then.'

Abbey saw the same kind of realization enter Ethan's face as he looked up at her. She
looked away from him and across at Karyn
with a look of anguish. 'It was a long time
ago.'

'Was that when you started hating me?'

She'd been so wrapped up in her grief that
she hadn't had much time to feel anything except loneliness. Hating him for not being there
had come later.

'I know it wasn't your fault now.'

Ethan could feel her pain across the room as if it were his own. The accident that had made him angry for so long made him even angrier for keeping him from her when she had needed him. A week ago he wouldn't have believed that he could have understood a complete stranger so very quickly. But somehow he just did.

He'd come to talk to her mother to get to know her better. There was no way he could have known that, in doing so, he would suddenly feel as if he already did. As if he'd known her his whole life. It knocked him sideways.

Without thinking, he stood up and walked to her in two steps. He waited until she looked up at him, then smiled softly. 'I'm here now.'

Her voice was low, choked, her words meant only for his ears. 'I don't know you now.'

He waited a second, then held out his hand in front of him. 'Hi, Abbey, I'm Ethan Wyatt.'

She looked down at his outstretched hand in the space between them, then back up into his soft eyes, her own eyes filled with questions.

'I have to leave real soon and I don't want to leave without knowing you.'

Abbey's heart threatened to push out of her chest. She knew she couldn't change her life now, couldn't erase the past. But maybe she *could* take the chance on healing some of the pain. Already, by his very presence, he'd started to build bridges in her life she would never have believed it possible to build.

With the slowest of movements she gradually outstretched her hand and felt it engulfed by his. 'Hello, Ethan.'

CHAPTER ELEVEN

ETHAN reached out and held her hand in his as they walked along the gravel driveway from her house. And Abbey let him.

A smile appeared on his face as he looked ahead. 'So where do we go from here?'

'Well...' She looked ahead as well. 'We could turn left and go into the town or I guess we could turn right and walk along the river.'

That wasn't what he'd meant. But he suspected she knew that. He swung their hands back and forth between them. 'River sounds good to me.'

Still looking ahead of them, Abbey smiled. If he continued swinging their hands that way it wouldn't surprise her in the least to find them skipping along the river. She risked a sideways glance and laughed when he did exactly the same thing at the same time. 'This is awkward as hell.'

'Yeah, I know.' He continued smiling. 'But it's a start.'

Their hands stopped swinging and she felt his fingers move against her skin. Her skin warmed. It felt good. It felt good, but she couldn't let it feel long-lasting. This was just a healing time they both had to go through, that was all.

They turned right at the stone gateposts.

'That's the first time you and your mom have had much of a talk, huh?'

'Yes, we've not exactly been best friends.'

'That mother-daughter thing.'

'I guess so.' She glanced at him again. 'But we've made a start now, thanks to you.'

He nodded. 'I'm glad about that.'

Their steps took them closer to the small lane to the river.

'Did we talk about your family much before?'

She nodded, glancing at their feet for a second. 'We talked about everything.'

'Life, the universe and all that?'

'Pretty much.'

'So there's not much point in my telling you about *my* family, is there?' He tugged her hand slightly less forcibly than he had a couple of days ago and steered them onto the lane.

'You could tell me about them now. How are your mom and dad, for instance?'

'They're good. Still mad about each other, still mad that none of us boys have made them grandparents. Though Jon is getting married in a few months so at least that's one of us tied down.' His smile was wry as he realized that technically his younger brother would be the second to get married. 'They don't know about you.'

Abbey shrugged. 'They wouldn't. You were going to tell them when you got back.'

'I got held up on that.'

'I know.'

The sound of flowing water filled their ears as they reached the river and started along the narrow path. Its width forced them to walk closer together so they would still fit side by side and Abbey felt a familiar tingle of awareness at his nearness.

Ethan moved his fingers along her skin again, fascinated by the soft warmth of her. It didn't feel awkward or out of place to touch her. It felt…normal. Right. As if he'd held her hand a thousand times.

He thought back to the conversation in the conservatory. 'Did we talk about having kids?'

Abbey's stomach twisted. She took a couple of breaths before answering. 'Yes.'

'And what did we think about that idea?'

'You wanted a baseball team.' She laughed softly at the memory. 'I talked you down some.'

'Damn.' He squeezed his fingers tighter. 'I always wanted a baseball team.'

'It took some persuading.'

There was a pause and then, 'I miss not knowing those things.'

Abbey looked at his profile as they continued along the path. She allowed herself the luxury of just looking at him. The pleasure that she felt inside at him being there, beside her. How many times had she dreamt about just this?

'How can you miss something you don't re-member?'

He was aware she was looking at him. As aware as he was of the fact that she was so close to him, her body occasionally brushing against his. But he was also aware of time. Of how little of it he had before he had to leave. And knowing that broke down the barriers that were normally present when he spent time with a woman. Getting to know someone normally happened at a much slower pace. Which meant that people had the time they needed to open up. For once he was just going to have to say things as they entered his head. It made things more intense but, he knew at the same time, necessary.

'I've always felt there was something miss-ing.' He smiled at the humour of his statement. 'Apart from my memory, I mean.'

She smiled back at his attempt at levity. 'People often feel that. It's a human emotion. It doesn't mean you somehow knew you missed our time together.'

'Maybe.' He allowed that there could be some truth in her words. 'But it makes more sense now that I know there was a you.'

Her heart beat a little faster.

'I'm not going to tell you I haven't dated.'

A twist, similar to the one she felt when she thought about Amy, crossed her stomach. 'It's only natural that you would have. I remember how popular you were with the other female leaders at the camp. I wasn't too well liked when you started paying attention to me.'

Ethan nodded. 'It's my height.'

'It's what?' Her mouth twitched.

He nodded again. 'Women like tall guys.' And shrugged. 'What can I say?'

The twitch promoted itself to a grin. 'Okay, you got me there, I probably wouldn't have looked twice if you'd been three feet tall.'

'I was cute when I was three feet tall.'

'I'll bet.'

They walked another while and Ethan's fingers moved again. Abbey tried to distract herself from the tingling the movement created. 'No one serious, then?'

'When I was three feet tall?'

'I already know about Maggie Blumfeld.'

Ethan's eyebrow quirked as he looked at her. 'I told you about Maggie?'

'Oh, yes.' She stopped and looked up at him. 'Your first crush, your first kiss. And she didn't staple your lips together like you thought she would.'

'And your first kiss?'

'Ah.' She looked up to the blue sky above them and smiled at the memory. 'Sean Donnelly. Waiting for the bus to school.'

His fingers tightened possessively around hers. 'And how did he rate?'

Her eyes sparkled when she looked into his. 'Somewhere between awful and bearable.'

Hazel eyes grew dark as he asked, 'And how did I rate?'

She damped her lips before answering. 'Somewhere between pretty good and pretty terrific.'

'Only pretty terrific? Not amazing or mind-blowing or knock-your-socks-off great?'

'You did okay.'

Ethan stepped towards her, his eyes growing even darker as his voice dropped. 'Well, I obviously needed more practise, then.'

'Oh, we practised.' Her pulse beat hard in her veins as she watched his head descend towards hers. 'We practised lots.'

'Maybe we should practise some more.' He smiled a slow, purely sexual smile. *'Abigail.'*

It crossed her mind for the briefest of seconds that she seemed to be constantly kissing Ethan, no matter what way she approached it. It just kept on happening.

But the simple fact was, she'd always loved kissing him. Because he went way beyond 'knock-your-socks-off great'.

His firm mouth touched against hers while his eyes still looked into hers. Then he released her hand and drew her body into his, his eyes closing simultaneously with hers. He waited the briefest of seconds and then moved his mouth against hers until she softened.

Abbey's hands snaked up around his neck and she used the leverage to pull him closer. It had been such a very long time since she'd kissed him without restraint, without holding back, or hiding how badly she wanted to kiss him.

She opened her mouth to him, allowed her tongue to dance in time with his, tasting and teasing. And it was there. Desire, wanting. Spiralling deep in her abdomen and warming her blood. It had only ever taken one kiss. The moment they had kissed she had always been set alight. And she'd never experienced that with anyone but Ethan. Never before him and never since.

A low moan escaped from deep in her throat and she tangled her fingers in the short hair at the nape of his neck. The deep-seated need for him was familiar too, but not just from the memories of all the times they'd made love, taken from and given pleasure to each other. It was familiar from the late-night dreams that had woken her from restless slumber with tangled sheets and a body damp with sweat. The times when she had woken alone in an empty bed filled with longing for something that was gone.

Ethan was stunned to his core by how quickly he wanted her. He could have taken her right there by the river's edge and had to fight hard to stop himself. But this wasn't the kind of woman he could have done that with. This was Abbey. This was Abbey who was new to him. He couldn't treat her like some quick fix, some sordid moment of release. Because she was Abbey. She meant something.

He dragged his mouth from hers, his breathing laboured as he looked down at her eyes. Eyes filled with the same desire he was experiencing. He swallowed hard. 'Okay. We really need to stop.'

She nodded slowly, if a little reluctantly. 'We probably should.'

'Probably best.' He continued to hold her close. 'What with being outdoors and all.'

Her smile was slow, potent and purely sexual. 'Not that that ever stopped us before.'

The words had an immediate effect on his body and he groaned with a recent memory, his eyes closing. 'That damn sex on the beach?'

'Uh-huh.'

Ethan swore under his breath before opening his eyes to look at her again. 'It was always like this with us, wasn't it? This chemistry.' He knew he'd asked her before, but he needed it confirmed again. Needed to hear it a hundred times so he knew it wasn't just him.

Her answer came out on a sigh, her eyes sad. 'Yes.'

He looked from one of her eyes to the other, seeing a wealth of memories as she added, 'Every single time.'

He tightened his hold on her, his hands moving against her back. 'How could I not remember something like that?'

The whispered words tugged her heart into a million shattered pieces. 'Maybe it's better that only one of us had that kind of torture.'

He opened his mouth to speak and was silenced when she swiftly removed a hand from his hair to place a finger over his mouth. 'Shh.'

His eyebrows raised in silent question.

Abbey smiled. It was the first time she'd felt even vaguely in control since his return. The age-old power game that women could play when they knew that a man wanted them. She wanted to hold onto that feeling for just a while.

With one hand still entangled in his hair she moved her hips against him. She felt his immediate reaction. She heard his groan and felt the whisper of it escape against her fingers.

'I used to dream about you.' She whispered the words as she looked up into his eyes. 'Until there was a time when I didn't know what had been a dream and what had been real.'

His hands moved against her back, moved down to push the material of her T-shirt up until he could touch her skin. He moved his fingers in hypnotic circles, barely making contact so that it felt like the far-off touches of her dream lover.

'I had to let go, Ethan, or you would have tortured me for ever. You need to understand that.'

He nodded slowly. He did understand. If he'd been in the same place she'd been he might even have done the same thing. Rather than have it affect the rest of his life.

She felt him kiss the finger against his mouth and she smiled at him, her eyes glowing. 'But we really do have this time to lay those ghosts to rest, don't we?'

Widening his eyes slightly, he said, 'Mmmf mm mff mm mm mm.'

Abbey laughed and removed her finger. 'Sorry, didn't quite catch that.'

'A lot can happen in a few days.'

It was true, it could. A lot had already happened in a few short days. Her life had changed and in a way, she surmised, Ethan's had too. They just had to take the next few days and heal the old wounds. Before they let go and went on with their lives. The lives, she kept reminding herself, that they now had on separate sides of an ocean.

CHAPTER TWELVE

'WE'RE in the kitchen.'

Abbey turned down the hallway at the sound of Karyn's voice. A little breathless from jogging home from town where she'd left Ethan, she tried to bring her breathing under control before facing them.

She glanced at the bottle of wine between them and the relaxed smiles on both their faces.

'Grilling everyone for information about my life now, are we, Mother?'

Her mother searched her face and found the teasing light in her eyes. Her shoulders seemed to relax. 'Your friend is most amusing. I'm enjoying her company.'

Abbey looked at Karyn with a smile. 'Oh, she's amusing, all right. That and a great many other things that make her simply adorable. I have excellent taste in friends.'

'And in husbands.' Karyn grinned from behind her wineglass. 'Speaking of which, where did you leave the hunky husband?'

She shook her head and moved to the cupboard to grab herself a glass. 'He went to the hotel to get changed. We're having dinner.'

'That's nice.' Elizabeth smiled in approval.

'I guess it is.' She reached for the bottle and shook it slightly. 'You two planning on getting sloshed?'

Karyn laughed. 'I'm hoping if your mother gets tight she'll spill all the info on her new guy.'

Elizabeth actually blushed, much to Abbey's amazement and amusement. 'I have no intention of getting either sloshed *or* tight, thank you very much.'

'Oh, go on, Mother, give it a bash. Karyn's a great teacher.'

'Hell, yes, Abbey here was teetotal 'til she met me. But I loosened her up some.'

'Well, I'll certainly sleep better knowing she has you to look out for her.'

Abbey understood better where her own sarcastic streak came from. Maybe she was more like her mother then she'd thought. It was a weird sensation. And not one she was entirely sure she was comfortable with just yet.

'Just don't go teaching my mother anything else apart from how to hold a drink or two, oh friend of mine.' She took a sip of wine and turned to leave the room. 'I'm going to have a shower and get changed.' She paused at the door to toss words over her shoulder: 'You two stay out of mischief.'

Karyn laughed. 'Just so long as you go out and make some with that husband of yours.'

She blushed as she walked up the stairs, muttering under her breath, 'Already done enough of that by the river, I think.'

The knock on her door twenty minutes later preceded the peek of her mother's head around its edge. 'Are you decent?'

'I'm dressed, if that's what you mean.'

She pushed the door open and walked in to sit on the end of Abbey's bed, watching as her daughter ran a brush through her hair. 'You look very nice.'

The brush halted its movement as she met her mother's eyes in the mirror. 'Thank you. Are you sloshed already?'

'No, not quite.' She smiled and Abbey wondered if all the recent practise was making it easier for her to do. She then fixed a more serious expression on her face. 'I wanted to talk to you about Ethan.'

She cringed inwardly. 'There's really not much to talk about.'

Elizabeth's reflection said she didn't really believe that. 'Are you very in love with him?'

'Mother—'

'Because I just wanted to tell you that I like him.'

'You only talked to him for five minutes.'

'It was a little longer than that.'

'Not long enough for you to know whether or not he's a wonderful guy.'

She nodded slightly. 'Maybe not. But you're my daughter and, even though we may not have figured out how to be friends, I think I know you well enough to know you wouldn't have married someone dreadful.'

If Abbey had believed her mother had that kind of faith in her judgement she might just have got around to telling her she was married all those years ago. Her eyes widened in surprise.

'Not that Paul isn't a nice chap too.' Elizabeth seemed to consider her own words where they hung in front of her face. Then she smiled at Abbey. 'But he certainly doesn't have the ''oomph'' factor that your Ethan does.'

Abbey stared as her mother emphasized the 'oomph' with a small, ladylike thrust of her fist. Words escaped her.

'You see, I do actually know something about that ''oomph'' factor.'

'Karyn just taught you that phrase, didn't she?'

Elizabeth grinned. 'Yes, as a matter of fact she did.'

Abbey shook her head. 'She's never visiting again.'

'Oh, I'm going to visit her in Dublin next weekend.' She focused on Abbey's face with a girlish smile. 'She's taking me out for the evening.'

'Like hell she is.'

She waved her hand back and forth in front of her. 'Anyhow, as I was saying. This ''oomph'' factor.' She smiled with a twinkle in her eyes. 'Your father had it by the bucketful.'

'Oh, my God. Please tell me you're not going to talk to me about your sex life.'

'I thought they taught you biology in school, dear.'

'Yes, yes, indeed they did.' Abbey's words came out in a rush. 'So there's no need for you to go into it with me. *Really.*'

'I had assumed you'd know something on the subject by your age.' She smiled at her daughter's look of outrage. 'I was just going to say that having someone in your life who can have that kind of an effect on you is a rare thing. Having someone with that effect who deeply cares for you as well is something that you just can't allow to pass by.'

Now her mother was giving her advice? She was going to need therapy after this week...

Turning round on her stool, she looked Elizabeth straight in the eye and sighed. 'Mother, I don't think you should get used to Ethan. He's leaving again soon. This is just—' She searched carefully for the right words. 'It's kind of a goodbye, I guess.'

The sadness must have been evident in her face because her mother immediately replied with a surprised, 'But why on earth is it, dear? There's nothing to stop you from going with him.'

Apart from the fact that he hadn't shown the slightest indication of wanting her to go with him. The thought, though obvious, still brought a frown to her face. But she couldn't go even if he had. 'I have a life here now. A career, a home.' She smiled at another reali-zation. 'And a mother to get to know.'

The older woman's face lit up. 'We can get to know each other regardless of where you decide to live. The important thing is that we start to make the effort.'

Her throat closed and she blinked at new tears. Was she ever going to stop crying?

'I know that. But Ethan and I have moved on from where we were when we ran off and got married. I can't change that any more than he can.'

'You can change anything if you want something badly enough. If you love him, Abbey, *really* love him...' she leaned forward with a soft smile '...then don't let him go.'

It vaguely flitted through her head that her mother had stopped calling her Abigail. It was a sign of the change in their relationship, maybe?

She thought of arguing her case but the hopeful look on her mother's face was more than she'd seen there in a long time. If ever. It couldn't hurt to lie a little to keep her smiling...

'I know, Mum.'

Ethan couldn't remember ever having felt so nervous and excited before a date. It was an intoxicating combination.

He really, *genuinely* couldn't wait to see her again, and she'd only left a matter of minutes beforehand. Was this what it had felt like before? If it was even a half of it then he could understand why he'd run off and got married that way. It had to have been one heck of a reason for him to risk his mom's wrath at having done her out of a wedding day. A grin spread across his face at the thought.

Abbey was just so much more than he could ever have imagined her being. Staring at a photograph for years would never have painted the picture he was now seeing up close. He'd always liked what he'd seen in the picture. He liked even more what he was glimpsing now.

Because it was just that. A glimpse. There were facets he hadn't even begun to touch on and he wondered if a few days were going to be enough time to discover them all...

Just as he started to realistically think about coming back again, there was a knock on his hotel door.

She hadn't left? He got to the door in three long strides, the wide grin fading slightly as he looked at Amy's face. 'Oh, hey.'

Amy's eyes widened slightly at the greeting. 'You were expecting someone else?'

He nodded. 'Sorry. I thought you might have been Abbey.'

'You mean A.J.'

'Yeah, I've got to used to calling her Abbey now I know her better.'

Amy walked into the room and turned round to look at him with questioning eyes. 'And you know her better now, do you? When did that happen?'

'It's been a busy day.' He smiled as he closed the door.

She studied him as he walked past her and pulled clothes from the wardrobe. 'You're going out again?'

'Yeah.' He looked apologetically over his shoulder. 'I'm sorry, Amy. I've abandoned you some, haven't I?'

'Well...' She shrugged. 'It's not a holiday we're on. I take it you're going to see her again?'

A nod confirmed her suspicions.

'We're still leaving in four days, though.'

'Unless I want to be declared AWOL we are. That much I haven't got a say in.'

Amy moved across to sit on the window-seat, her eyes watching his every movement. 'So what are you doing?'

He glanced at her for a brief second. 'What do you mean?'

'I mean I thought we were here so you could get some answers about your missing months and then sort out the divorce paperwork before we leave.'

Ethan thought about the papers in his case. The practical side of him had brought them along, as if by bringing them he could justify the trip. He hadn't allowed himself to think for a second that he might find out he liked his wife. Or to imagine in his lifetime he would be so fiercely attracted to a stranger in a matter of hours.

Both of them were confessions he wasn't quite ready to make to Amy, though. 'I am getting answers about the missing months.'

'But having those answers still isn't going to bring Jamie back, is it?'

The old ache gripped him from low in his belly. The fact that he'd barely considered Jamie since he'd started to get involved with Abbey hit him with the force of a blunt punch. And there it was again. The guilt.

'No, it isn't.'

'Is it going to stop you from blaming yourself that he died?'

He avoided looking directly at her. 'I don't want to talk about this right now.'

Amy sighed. 'Because it's easier to hide behind running around after your *wife*?'

The sarcasm in her pronunciation of the word 'wife' drew his eyes to hers. He frowned hard. 'What exactly are you hinting at here, Amy?'

'I think that somewhere deep down you're trying to make amends for what happened. Maybe you're even trying to justify the fact that you lived when he didn't. Because we both know you've not dealt with that.'

'And how exactly *would* I deal with that?'

She ignored the rise of his voice. They'd had many an argument over the years so

Ethan's temper didn't phase her. 'By looking for some magical love affair to ease the pain and make things feel better?'

He swore vehemently, throwing clothing down on the bed before running a hand through his hair. 'You think that's what I'm doing here? You of all people think I'm some romantic idiot who's come running to look for the love of his life? If you thought that, then why didn't you just nail my feet to the ground at home?'

'I would have done.' She frowned back at him as her own voice rose. 'But you were so damned determined to come here!'

'Because I wanted to meet her! Wouldn't you have done the same thing if you'd found out you were married?'

With a breath she avoided his eyes and leaned back against the glass. A tense silence invaded the room before she answered, 'Ethan, I don't know what you felt when you ran off and got married. But I know that whatever it was it's gone. You don't remember it and you never will.' She looked back at him. 'I'm just worried you're reaching for something that doesn't exist any more.'

'What if it does?' The words spilled out before he could stop them and his eyes widened in surprise when they did. Did he even believe that?

Amy stared back at him in shock. 'What do you mean?'

He hadn't even reasoned it out in his own mind so discussing it with Amy didn't exactly feel like the best of plans. He took a breath and sat down beside his clothes. Eventually he looked back at her, having done an intense study of his feet. 'I don't know.'

'I think you do. Or you wouldn't have said it.'

He managed a shrug, his eyes searching up the wall above her head and onto the ceiling, looking for answers. 'Maybe there is something still there.'

'After all this time has passed by? You can't believe that.' She leaned forwards. 'Doesn't she have a fiancé now?'

'She hasn't said she'll marry him.'

Amy laughed slightly. 'I'd say already being married might be the problem there.'

'Maybe not loving him might be the problem.' And somehow he knew the words were true. She might not be in love with *him* any more, but he didn't believe she was in love with Paul either.

'This is crazy. Has she said she loves *you*?'

'No, she hasn't.' She'd said she'd loved him, past tense. But she'd also said the person she'd loved had died in the accident. She hadn't said she still had feelings for him now.

But she had said he'd haunted her. That she was tortured by dreams of them together. And she'd wanted him by that river as much as he'd wanted her. That all had to mean something, didn't it?

But was he grasping at straws to ease the pain he carried about Jamie? Was that why he felt the pull to Abbey so strongly and so damned fast? Was he really just searching for a cushion of some kind?

He couldn't do that to her, if that was what he was subconsciously searching for.

Amy saw his shoulders slump a barely perceptible inch. She knew him well enough to read the signs and she softened at the sight. 'I'm sorry, Ethan. I've always been straight with you.'

'I know you have.' He took another deep breath. 'And you're right. She hasn't said she's still in love with me. And we *are* both different people from the ones we were then.'

Ethan knew he'd changed since the accident. How could he not have? A person didn't live through an experience like that, didn't lose someone who'd been such a big part of their life beforehand, and *not* go through changes. His family had noticed it; Amy had noticed it. He knew it was true. All that coming to Ireland had shown him was that the woman he had married was an amazing person. It hadn't changed anything else.

'You need to let go of the past.'

He nodded. 'I know.' Then he glanced at her from beneath dark lashes. 'But I still need time to do that.'

Amy frowned at him again.

'We're still going back on schedule. Don't worry about it. I won't come back after I leave.'

CHAPTER THIRTEEN

SOMETHING had changed in the couple of hours since Abbey had left Ethan.

She studied his face across the table from her and tried to see just what it was. He still looked absolutely drop-dead gorgeous. It had been obvious since his return that that much hadn't changed in eight years, let alone a couple of hours.

She felt her body warm as he looked up at her. Memories of the afternoon made her mouth go dry and her pulse race before he glanced away.

And that was what was different. A small frown formed a crease between her eyes as she made the discovery. He couldn't look her in the eye.

'Okay, so are you going to tell me?'

He pushed the food around on his plate with the end of his fork. 'Tell you what?'

'What's wrong.'

'There's nothing wrong.' He glanced up and away again. 'The food's great.'

'I wasn't talking about the food.' She leaned her head closer and lowered her voice. 'You can't look at me for more than five seconds. So what's up?'

He was surprised by how well she had read him. It wasn't something he was used to people he didn't know that well doing. But then plenty of things had surprised him about Abbey.

Forcing himself to make eye contact and hold it, he raised an eyebrow at her. 'It's nothing.' He smiled. 'Really. I guess I'm just tired.'

She also recognized a lie. 'And now you're lying to me, aren't you?'

He took a breath. 'Do you know how disconcerting it is having you know me this well when I still don't really know you? Because it is.'

'And you're uncomfortable with that?'

'Well, like you said, it's not like we're the same people we were before.'

Abbey leaned back in her seat when he used her own words against her. Something had definitely changed and she needed to know the hell why.

'You've obviously been thinking about something since I left you.'

Ethan gritted his teeth as she continued reading him. But he was the one who had pushed to open the can of worms, wasn't he? Now he had to figure out a way to close it again.

'I had a bit of a talk with Amy, that's all.'

Abbey felt the newly familiar pang of jealousy at the mention of the other woman's name. It grated that she was such a part of his life. Would it have grated as much if she'd met her when she'd been together with Ethan before? Would they have been friends? The fact was she would never know one way or another. The fact was, she didn't like her in the here and now.

'About me?'

He nodded. 'Yeah, about you. And about me.'

'And about you and me?'

'Is there a you and me?'

The question knocked her out of synch for a second. But she recovered quickly. 'There was. And she doesn't like that, does she?'

It hadn't occurred to him in quite that sense. 'I guess she doesn't.'

Abbey smiled. 'I'll bet.'

Ethan felt a more genuine smile appear. 'There's that jealousy thing again.'

She sighed, considering a sarcastic retort and instead opting for a little honesty. 'Apparently so.'

The confession surprised him. 'You're admitting you're jealous?' He continued smiling at the warning glare she directed at him. 'Wow. That's a step for you.'

'I'll admit I'm jealous of the fact that she was there at a time I should have been.'

That made sense. But he continued smiling nevertheless. He liked that she was jealous.

'That's not her fault any more than it is either of ours.'

'Does she love you?'

'I'd say so. We've been friends a long time.'

Abbey avoided the direct gaze that moments before he'd been unable to hold. 'And do you love her?'

'Yes.' He waited for a split second before adding in a softer voice, 'But not in the way you're asking me.'

The sense of relief was immediate. Easing the pang of jealousy somewhat. She smiled at the softness in his voice, the fact that he had somehow understood she needed to hear his words. 'Do you know that's not the way *she* feels?'

Ethan considered her words carefully even when he wanted to answer with an immediate 'no'. But there had been times, this last year, when he'd caught Amy looking at him when she'd thought he hadn't noticed. Or when she'd smiled a certain way. It had created a sense of there being something different, new. But it had also made him slightly uncomfortable, so he'd done the manly thing and chosen to ignore it.

'I guess you'd have to ask her that.'

Abbey nodded. 'I guess I would, right enough.'

Ethan watched her as she broke eye contact with him and glanced around the room. He'd thought long and hard about the things that Amy had said to him. Searched his heart hard to see if she was right. But how could he know if he was doing something subconsciously?

The truth remained that he wasn't some great romantic fool who ran round the world searching for someone to complete his life. He'd never believed that another person could do that. A soul mate, if there was such a thing, should add to a person's life. Not complete it. Because if they weren't complete in themselves, then how could they hope to make a relationship that important work?

Which had brought him to the question of whether or not he believed himself to be a complete person...

'I took a long time to wake up after the accident.'

Abbey's eyes were drawn back to his face as he spoke.

He smiled a small smile. 'They didn't know if I would at all. Told my family to expect the worst and get there quick.'

Her heart tore again at the thought he might have died. She wouldn't have been able to bear it.

'But I woke up. And eventually I started to realize where I was. I knew the people around me, knew I was in a hospital.' He shrugged. 'Knew I hurt like hell.'

She stared as he paused, as if waiting for her to say something. But she couldn't. She could only listen.

'When they took all the tubes and stuff out and I could talk, I got to ask what had happened. At first they just told me I'd been in an accident.' He took a breath and frowned down at his plate as he added, 'It took nearly two months for them to tell me about Jamie.'

Abbey reached her hand across to his and tangled her fingers with his longer ones when his hand turned over. She squeezed gently, transmitting to him that she understood how it must have felt to be told.

'You always hear stories about people who live through an accident when someone else dies. How they feel guilt for having lived. I guess you never get to really understand how that feels 'til it happens to you.'

'Do you still feel guilty?' She squeezed his fingers again and he looked up at her.

'Yeah, I do.' His mouth quirked at the words. 'And it took a few sessions of post-trauma counselling to get those words out that easy, I can tell you.'

'You'll have been angry too.'

'Mad as hell.'

'At Jamie?'

He smiled at her insight and tangled his fingers in and out of hers, looking down at their hands as he did. 'At Jamie, at the truck driver, at myself. I got madder when I started physical therapy and my body wouldn't work like it used to, but at least that gave me somewhere to focus my energy. Amy got the brunt of all that emotion practically every day, and she still stuck around.'

Abbey tried hard to ignore the jealousy that Amy had been there. Instead, as she studied the dark hair on Ethan's head she tried to focus on the fact that without Amy's help Ethan might not have made it through those long, tough months. She should feel grateful that he'd had someone there when she couldn't be there herself. Amy, in a way, had made it possible for Ethan to walk back to Abbey. And Abbey knew in her heart she was very glad that had happened. Despite all the last few days had brought her.

'I'm glad you had someone like her there, that you weren't alone.'

His eyes rose to meet hers and a slow smile appeared. 'She's been a hell of a friend to me, Abbey, and I wouldn't change that.'

'I wouldn't ask you to.'

'But the fact that she was there through it means that she was the one I talked to and that means she knows me pretty well.'

A sense of foreboding grew in Abbey's stomach.

'And right now she thinks I'm spending time with you for the wrong reasons.'

Her breath caught in her chest before she managed to ask, 'And do you think you are?'

He looked down at their joined hands and reluctantly freed his fingers and placed his hand in his lap. 'I didn't think so until we talked.'

'But now you're not sure.'

Hazel eyes blinked once, twice, and then he replied, 'I don't know.'

She stared at him, felt him distancing himself even further than the removal of his hand. And it hurt. It *really* hurt.

Ethan watched her with guarded eyes as she curled her fingers into her palm and slowly drew her hand back across the table. Before she looked away from him he even saw the flash of pain in her eyes. And seeing her pain hurt him. He frowned hard. 'I don't know what I expected when I decided to come here. Maybe Amy's right and I expected that piecing together the missing months would help me make more sense of what happened.'

Abbey nodded, not managing to look at him. 'We both needed closure on that time in our own ways. That makes sense.'

Hesitating for a second he leaned closer, his voice low. 'But I didn't expect to be this attracted to you.'

Her traitorous eyes moved back to lock with his.

'What happened today is more than I could ever have expected.'

Her traitorous body warmed at the memory.

'I want you. I wanted you by that river and, if I'm honest, I still do.'

Her traitorous heart skipped a few beats in hope.

'But I won't hurt you again, not knowing I'm doing it. I'm still gonna get on that plane and I'm still gonna go back to my life.'

Her punishment came in the words she'd already known were the truth. But somehow hearing them out loud made it more real to her. He was leaving. She would have to let go of

Ethan. She had thought that would lead to a healing of sorts. It wasn't supposed to lead to more pain.

She nodded.

Ethan frowned at her acceptance of what he was saying. When he wanted her to do—what? Tell him she didn't want him to leave? Didn't want him out of her life? The fact that she was giving in so easily meant it really had been over for her for a long time. But he should have known that, shouldn't he? So why did he feel angry about it?

'You're the one who keeps telling me that you have a life now, and that I don't know you, and you're right. I don't know you.'

'No, you don't.' Or he'd have known he was breaking her heart all over again.

'And even though I want to, I can't get to know you better if the only reason I'm doing it is to look for a cure to something that you can't fix for me.'

She frowned at him. 'Is that what *Amy* said you were doing?'

'Amy's entitled to her own opinions. All she did was force me to think this through.' His anger grew when he felt the need to defend what he was saying. 'If this thing we had was meant to be, then you'd have fought harder to find out what happened before now, don't you think? But you didn't do that, Abbey. You let it go.'

Dark eyes widened as he threw the last words at her. She stared at him, the man whom she'd loved for so long that having her heart broken by him had shadowed everything she'd done in her life since the day she'd met him. How could he believe that she hadn't wanted what they'd had enough to fight for it?

'Maybe I let go because I knew deep down it was over.'

Ethan leaned back in his seat and stared back at her. Well, that was that then, wasn't it? If he'd held any subconscious hope that spending time with her might make them both remember they loved each other and thereby fix all the hurt and lead to a happily ever after, then his subconscious had its answer.

Taking a breath, he looked around the room at other couples smiling at each other across their tables. He watched a family laugh and a couple of kids run around and he felt lonelier than he had in his entire life.

'I'm not sorry I met you, Abbey.' He glanced over at her face. 'I want you to know that.'

Abbey drew on every reserve of self-control she possessed to stop herself from crying again. 'Thank you.'

'No, I owe *you* the thanks.' He lifted a napkin from his lap and placed it on his uneaten food. 'Because at least now I know what I did with my missing months.'

Her focus pinpointed the napkin on his plate. 'Yes, I suppose you do.' She frowned as she looked up into his face. 'I hope it helps.'

After a breath he merely nodded at their plates. 'Dinner's on me; I'll charge it to my room.'

'Thank you.'

She watched as he pushed his chair back from the table and stood, his eyes avoiding hers. She bit her inner lip hard as he turned away from her.

Then he stopped and looked back, his eyes telling her that thoughts were running through his mind. He pursed his lips and shook his head.

'Just so you know, though, if it'd been switched round, I'd never have stopped trying to find you.'

Her breath caught.

'If something that good came along I'd have done anything to have one more moment of it.' He leaned in closer, his hands resting on the table. 'Because then, if I *did* let it go, I'd have known I did it because I chose to. Not because some random twist of fate took it from me.'

CHAPTER FOURTEEN

ABBEY was cold. Chilled right down to the bone on what was a mild evening. And there was no other explanation for her chill except that she was walking away from Ethan.

Hugging her arms around her body, she walked up the dark street towards home. His words echoed in her ears while hot, angry tears flowed down her cheeks.

Damn him.

Damn him for making her cry every day since he'd walked into her damned birthday party. Damn him even more that, for the briefest of time during the day, he had actually managed to give her a tiny flicker of hope.

Because it had been there. She might have denied it to herself and to everyone else around her, but when they had started to talk that afternoon she had felt the tiniest hope that things might just be going to be okay.

Ethan had felt everything she'd felt in their heated kisses by the river. She hadn't been alone there. He wanted her, even said so himself. As she walked further away from him with each step that need was still with her.

She'd worked so very hard at trying to forget him. Had built a life for herself without him. But that tiny flicker of hope his being there had created had shown her that all she'd actually been doing was filling in time. Trying to fill the gap that was left in her life.

Should she have fought harder? The thought stopped her in her tracks and she looked around the deserted street for answers. Had it really been her own stupid stubbornness that had stopped her from reaching out to hold onto what had meant so much? Had she broken her own heart by doubting what he had felt for her?

All it had taken in the end to bring him back to her was one letter. One letter that she had taken eight years to write.

She had gone through every doubt about her own ability to be loved so intensely by someone like Ethan. Had allowed the reality of everyday life as she knew it to crush her belief in happily ever after. And she'd been punishing herself for that mistake for years.

When all it would have taken would have been for her to reach out a little further. To have taken a chance. That way, she could have known if it was worth fighting for.

Ethan was right.

The tears stopped. *Ethan was right.*

If she had taken a chance and fought for what she'd wanted, she wouldn't have had to live with dozens of 'what ifs'. If she'd found him and made the effort to hold onto him and it still hadn't worked, she'd have had closure for a long time. Or she might even have won the million-dollar prize and spent those eight years with the man she'd loved with all of her heart and soul. But she'd taken their possibilities from them more surely than the driver of a truck had.

She only had herself to blame for her own broken heart.

The sudden clarity of it all made sense of everything her life was now and had been. Yes, she had a great career, a home and now, thanks to Ethan, the possibility of a closer family life. But she wasn't in love with Paul; she wasn't going to marry him even if she hadn't already been married. Because Paul wasn't the one great love of her life. Ethan Wyatt was. And she'd married him without a second's thought. Because it had been the most perfectly right thing she'd ever done.

And now he was leaving her. She would never see him again, hear his deep voice or hold his hand in hers. He'd been able to build a life because he didn't remember his life with her in it. It wasn't his fault he didn't or couldn't miss something he didn't know he'd had. For that reason, and out of love, she knew she had to let him go. But she also knew that the Ethan of now wanted her, physically if nothing else.

And she knew without a single doubt that having had something so good in her life, she would do anything to have one more moment of it. Just as he'd said.

She needed that one more moment.

Ethan paced the floor in his room, a restlessness driving his steps. He knew he'd just said goodbye to Abbey.

It had been the right thing to do. After all, he was still unsure of his motives for having pushed his way into her life these last few days. But knowing it was right didn't make it feel any better.

It didn't take away the ache he felt and it sure as hell didn't make him feel any less lonely.

She was a stranger. He didn't know how she took her coffee or how she liked her eggs in the morning. None of those little things that told a person they really knew another person and certainly none of the bigger things.

But before he'd got her letter he'd only been haunted by a face in a photograph and a few missing months of his life. Now he sorely suspected he would be a great deal more haunted by the Abbey he'd met, the one his body wanted so badly.

And now that he'd let her go he wanted her so badly it was tearing him apart.

He stopped pacing and looked at his own reflection in the mirror. What was he doing?

He might not know or remember Abbey, but he knew himself. If he'd married her and taken the 'for better or worse' vow, then he'd done it because he'd believed she was the one for him. He'd felt he couldn't live without her. That he'd wanted to spend the rest of his life with her. How could he know whether or not he'd made the right decision then if he didn't take a chance now?

As he'd left her he'd told her that if he'd found something that good he would have done anything for one more moment of it. And he wanted that. He wanted that extra moment, even if it was all he could have or was meant to have.

With widening eyes at his reflection he realized he was going to find her.

The knock on his door sounded as his hand grasped the knob. He hauled it open and looked down into her dark eyes.

'Abbey.'

'I want that one moment, Ethan.'

He couldn't have lied to her even if he'd wanted to. Knowing what he did of her now had taught him that her coming to him, saying those words, had taken a lot. And how could he have lied in the face of that, even if he hadn't already made his decision seconds ago to go to her?

'I want it too.'

She blinked up at him, her heart's beating stopping as she held her breath. 'Do you?'

'Yes.' The word came out on a strangled whisper as he reached out towards her, drawing her into his arms and into his room. 'I was coming to find you.'

'You were?' She frowned at her own amazing way with words. But what she would say when she saw him again hadn't been thought out any further than her introductory line. Her heart had led her back to him, not some portion of her brain that controlled witty repartee.

Ethan looked down into the face that was so familiar to him now and smiled warmly at her look of uncertainty. 'I still can't tell you why I'm so drawn to you. I wish I could make sense of it, for you as well as for me. But the one thing I do know is that I can't stay away. You'll have to be the one to tell me to go.'

Her heart decided to beat again, this time in an erratic rhythm. She just couldn't find words. Instead she shook her head.

He squeezed his arms tighter around her and lowered his head to hers. It was enough to know that she wanted him there. Had still felt the need to come back to him even when he'd sent her away. Maybe there was no need to ask why or how or to dig deeper to discover why he'd made this trip in the first place. As his mouth met hers and he felt the sigh of breath against his lips he knew that this was what he wanted. It was just that simple.

She smoothed her hands up across his wide chest and around his neck, drawing him as close as she could. There was no point in fighting against needing him. It was wasted energy. This was what she wanted. To be with Ethan, held safe by Ethan. There was nothing else in the room with them beyond that. Not in her mind. And the future could just wait. Because this time was theirs and nothing could take that from her.

He spent long, slow moments devouring her with his mouth, learning the taste of her. He moved his body against hers to learn how they fitted. The spark of passion was as instantaneous as it had been every other time they'd kissed, his body remembering what his mind couldn't. Hands moved against the soft material of her dress, then up to the rounded back to the softer feel of her skin. She felt warm, smooth, smelled deliciously female, and he was hooked.

Even as she moved her hands from the nape of his neck to fumble at the buttons of his shirt, she was aware of his hands on her body. She remembered only too vividly what they'd been like together. When they'd lain in a tangled maze of limbs and sheets that only Ethan had ever seemed able to negotiate. And she smiled a sexual smile against his mouth at the memories.

'What is it?' Whispering, his mouth remained against hers as he opened his eyes to look at her face.

She continued smiling as she opened her eyes, taking a moment to focus with his face so close to hers. 'This I remember.' She spoke against his lips.

Freeing one hand from the addictive touch of her skin, he leaned his head back enough to allow his fingers to trace the side of her face with his knuckles. 'Show me.'

Abbey felt heat rise in her cheeks at his intense stare. 'I'm not sure I remember enough to keep us occupied for a whole night.'

Ethan could read the question in her words, the small doubt that he wanted her to stay that long. He moved his knuckles over her swollen mouth, his eyes dark. 'Then I'll have to see if I can make some new memories for us.'

*   *   *

Karyn was waiting for her when she eventually wandered through the front door.

She raised an eyebrow at her smiling face and crossed her arms across her chest. 'Dirty stop-out.'

Abbey's smile grew into a grin before she giggled. 'Yep, that would be me.'

'I needn't ask where you've been all night.'

'Nope, you needn't.' She slipped off her heels and dangled them between her fingers as she moved towards the stairs. 'I'll just let your imagination go to work.'

Karyn's eyes followed her movement up two steps before she halted her progress. 'Paul rang.'

Abbey's feet stopped. She closed her eyes for a second, a pang of guilt crossing the region of her chest. 'When?'

'Last night, and again this morning.'

She turned her head and looked down at her friend. 'Where did you tell him I was?'

'I didn't. I just said you weren't here.' She stepped forward and leaned her arms on the banister. 'Honey, you have nothing to feel guilty about. He's bound to know that your relationship the way it was wasn't exactly solid.' She paused. 'What did you tell him before he left?'

'That I'd understand him not waiting for me. That I needed time. That kind of stuff.'

'That's as good as a split-up, then.'

'Except I didn't exactly say we were over, or tell him that I'm still in love with Ethan.'

Karyn's eyes widened at the ease with which she made the confession. 'You *know* now that you're definitely still in love with Ethan? No doubts?'

Abbey smiled a small, sad smile. 'Yes. For all the good it'll probably do me.' She would never have spent the night with him if she hadn't known it.

'And Ethan?' She asked the obvious.

The initial answer was a shrug. 'He still has to leave in a few days.'

'You didn't tell him.'

Dark eyes glanced away and then back. 'I didn't tell him.'

'You bloody idiot!'

She stared at her friend's outburst, a frown appearing. Karyn had never raised her voice to her in that way in the entire time they'd been friends. 'What exactly do you expect me to do, Karyn? I can't change the fact that he has to leave.'

Karyn frowned back at her. 'You could try just once opening your mouth and saying how you feel. You don't know that that wouldn't change things.'

'I know it won't stop the army from expecting him to report back at the end of his leave.'

'No, but you don't know that he won't want you to go with him, or that he won't want to come back.'

The very fact that he'd come back at all was more than she could ever have hoped for. The faint chance that they might still have a future after one wondrous night together was more than she was prepared to allow her heart to hope for.

'If he wanted either of those things he'd say so.'

Karyn made a grunt of disbelief. 'Oh, yes, like you have? It's easier to put the onus on somebody else, isn't it?'

Abbey shook her head. 'I'm not having this conversation with you when you're like this.'

'Because you know I'm right.'

She ignored her and kept walking upwards, one step at a time.

When Karyn realized she was being ignored she cleared her throat and tossed words upwards at her. 'We have to go back to Dublin, Abbey. Today.'

CHAPTER FIFTEEN

ABBEY stopped and turned to look down at her friend's bowed head. 'What do you mean we have to go back?'

'The Westside promotion is going pear-shaped. Paul needs us both back in the office today.'

The promotion of Westside's new sports wear had been in the pipeline for six months. Abbey's first big deal and one that stood to make Paul's company a great deal of money. She stunned herself in the knowledge that something that had been so important a week ago hadn't even entered her mind for days.

'Pear-shaped how, exactly?' She moved back down the stairs.

Karyn shrugged. 'The venue has the offer of a bigger-paying booking and the caterers have pulled out.'

'We'll never get caterers that good at short notice.' And the venue had been part of the selling point to the client in the first place. 'I'll have to ring them.'

'Paul has tried that. And the venue wants to speak to you in person, apparently, because you're the one they've been dealing with all along. That's what Paul pays you the big money for, right?'

Abbey might have admitted to herself she was no longer in a personal relationship with Paul, but he was still her boss. She'd had reservations about even getting involved with him outside the office for fear of it not working. And now she was about to have those reservations put to the test, wasn't she?

When Ethan left she was going to have to go back to her life. Still earn a living and pay her bills. The reality of her everyday existence was still going to have to have its demands attended to.

Her real world was rearing its ugly head. The veil of the dream world that had shrouded her realistic side was pulled back causing the same clarity of mind she'd experienced when she'd realized she'd needed that 'one more moment' with Ethan.

She couldn't lose her job at the same time as the love of her life. *Something* was going to have to be salvaged.

Blinking her eyes, she focused on the wooden banister at her side. 'Then we'll have to go back.'

Karyn nodded slowly as she looked at her. 'I knew you'd say that.'

Abbey turned to go back up the stairs.

'What about Ethan?'

She stopped for a second, looking upwards. 'I've got to try and sort this quickly enough to come back to say goodbye.' She turned her head with a sad smile, her heart breaking. 'I knew I was going to have to get back to my life, Karyn. This is just fate's way of kicking me up the backside to get me to do it.'

'You'll tell him where you're going, though?'

She nodded. 'I'll try and talk to him before we leave, but he's going to spend some time with Amy today.' The jealousy gripped her again as she thought of the talk he'd said he was going to have with her. He'd made little of it and had held her in his arms as he'd told her it would be okay. But it still tore that she was leaving him with her. With a wry smile she realized she would have to get used to the idea. Because by the end of the week, Amy would still be a part of his life. 'So if he's not there I'll leave him a message to let him know I'll be back before he goes.'

'I'm going home, Ethan.' Amy looked across at him as they walked through the forest trail to an ancient waterfall. Ethan had suggested they do at least one touristy thing while in Ireland. 'Come with me.'

Ethan frowned slightly as he looked ahead of them. 'The flight isn't for another three days.'

'I rang the airline and we can change our tickets. We could go home for a couple of days before you have to go back to base.'

He took a deep breath. 'I'm not going early, Amy. I'm staying here.'

Stopping, she turned and looked at him. 'Why?'

The sunshine beat down on his face as he looked upwards. Then he turned and took another breath before making his big confession. 'I think I'm falling in love with her.'

Amy's eyes widened. 'How in hell can you think that? You've hardly met her.'

'Apparently there isn't a time allowed on feeling something for someone.'

'No.' She shook her head. 'You only think this because you believe there's a history there. You're grasping at straws.'

He mirrored her head movement. 'No, I don't think I am. And technically there is a history there.'

'And you can stand there and tell me that none of this has to do with how you feel about losing Jamie.'

Ethan had thought about that quite a bit since Abbey had left his arms that morning. She'd hardly been gone five minutes and he had felt the ache of her leaving. As if she'd taken a part of him with her. It was something he couldn't remember ever having experienced before. Couldn't remember. But he felt it anyhow.

'I can't bring Jamie back. I've known that for a long time.' His words were soft as his feet turned back along the pathway. 'And a part of me will probably always wonder why I lived when he didn't.'

She followed him. 'You think it was because you were meant to be with Abbey.'

'I think it's possible.'

'Why does there even have to *be* some big reason? It was an accident. That's why they're called *accidents*. They just happen. You were lucky.'

'Was I?' he asked with a small laugh, glancing at her when she caught up with his longer strides. 'There have been times when I've wondered about that. Jamie didn't have to stay behind and go through all this stuff.'

'He didn't get to live the rest of his life. He won't ever get to know who he could have been or what he could have done.'

'I've been thinking about that too.' He stopped and ran a hand back through his hair, ruffling it, then smoothing his palm down over his face. 'And that's sorta what made up my mind about this.'

Amy watched as he uncovered his face and looked at her. She watched cautiously as he stepped forward and placed his large hands on her shoulders. 'I don't understand.' It was the first time in their long friendship she hadn't.

Ethan nodded with a small smile. 'I know you don't. I'm not entirely sure I do either, but it's how I feel.'

She stared up into his eyes.

He continued explaining. 'I owe it to Jamie to find out who I could be, what I might do with the rest of my life.'

His words made sense even though she didn't want to hear where they were taking him.

'And in order to do that I have to be open to the possibilities.'

'Like the possibility that you married the right woman?'

He continued to smile, his eyes sparkling at her. 'Could be. I just know I can't stay away from her. That has to mean something.'

Amy's shoulders slumped beneath his hands. She knew he meant what he was saying, could see in his eyes that he felt it. She couldn't fight him when he was this determined. And in a way it took a weight from her shoulders to know that he was moving on. Wasn't it what she'd wanted him to do for a long time now?

Another weight removed from her shoulders as his hands worked their way into the pockets of his jeans. 'I haven't talked to Abbey about it, but after I leave I'm hoping she'll come and spend some time with me or let me come back again. I need to know where we're going.'

Amy started to walk along the path again. 'Is she dumping her guy?'

He felt his stomach clench at the very thought of her with that other guy. He hadn't liked it from the start and he hated it now. But surely she wouldn't have spent the night in his arms if she intended staying with someone else. What they had shared had been too good for him to let himself believe that of her. 'I certainly hope so.'

Amy raised an eyebrow in his direction.

'She doesn't love him.'

'And again I'll ask, has she said she still loves you?'

'No.' He walked beside her. 'But she did once. And I'm gonna have a damn good try at having her remember what that felt like.'

'I hope you're right, Ethan.'

They walked several more steps before he waded in and asked, 'Do you?'

She stopped and stared at him. 'What does that mean?'

It seemed to be the week for sorting out the relationships in his life. 'Do you hope she's really in love with me? Can you honestly say you're pleased that I'm falling for her?'

Amy grew flustered. 'I haven't any idea what you mean by that.'

'I think you do, Amy.' He frowned at the thought that what he was doing could push away the one true friend he'd had these last few years. 'You've given up a ton of your own life for me these last years. Don't you want a life with someone special too?'

'I haven't given up anything. I've spent time with someone I care about and that's what matters.'

Ethan noted how she avoided his gaze and he knew, he just knew. 'Amy.' His voice was soft. 'I can never repay everything you've done for me since the accident. You have to know how I feel about you.'

Her eyes looked up into his in question.

He felt bad about what he was going to say. But it needed saying. 'But you also have to know I've always seen you as a sister. I want you to go out there and find that someone for you. Because I love you and I want you to be happy. And I don't think you can be when you keep hanging around me and all my big problems.'

Looking away from him, she cleared her throat and answered. 'You needed me.'

Ethan nodded. 'Yes, I did. And you were there. But now it's okay for you to have a life of your own.'

Her eyes blinked hard in the bright light. 'So I should just never see you again, never call or write? Forget you exist?'

'I hope not. I want you in my life; I just don't want you to feel your life has to revolve around me.'

She frowned at him, her eyes glistening. 'Because I don't agree with your relationship with Abbey?'

'No.' He stepped closer to look down into her face. 'Because I don't think it's fair for me to keep using you as some kind of crutch. I know plenty of guys who have wanted to get close to you and you've blown them all off, and I don't want to feel guilty that you've done that because you think you should always be there for me.'

'I did it because I love you.'

His heart twisted when her voice cracked on the words. 'I know. But I can't give you what you should have, Amy. You need to find someone who can love you in the way you should be loved.'

Amy looked away from him again, hiding her eyes. And Ethan knew without her saying it that she knew he'd guessed what she felt ran deeper than friendship. He might not have been able to follow the honourable path when it came to confusing Abbey's life, but he could follow it with Amy. She was his friend; he owed it to her to set her free.

'I can't just disappear out of your life, Ethan.'

He understood that better than ever after this week. 'I don't want you to. I still need my friend. I just want to give you more space, that's all. I'll still be here for you.'

She nodded as she managed to look back at him. 'And I will for you, you know that.'

He did. He smiled at her as he pulled his hands from his pockets and reached out to pull her into a hug. 'I do know that, sweetheart. This isn't a goodbye.'

Her voice was muffled from his T-shirt. 'You're just sorting *everything* out on this trip, aren't you?'

'Yeah, I guess I am. Maybe it's just time, that's all.'

'That Abbey better know what she has.'

'I hope so.'

CHAPTER SIXTEEN

THE fact that she hadn't been able to find him preyed on Abbey's mind the whole way to Dublin.

She'd searched the whole of Killyduff, what there was of it, and hadn't found even a glimpse of him. So she'd been forced to leave a note for him at the hotel desk.

Writing it had brought a sense of unease. One that grew as the countryside gave way to wider roads and more traffic as she got closer to the city.

The turns on familiar roads brought her concentration back to driving. She'd convinced Karyn it would be better if they both brought their own cars back. That way she could drive back the minute she'd fixed the problems with the Westside promotion. It didn't enter her head for a second that she wouldn't be able to sort them. She might not have been much good with her personal life, but she was hell on legs when it came to her job.

Having eventually negotiated the heavy traffic, she pulled into the multi-storey car park beside her workplace and took a moment to calm herself. She was nervous about seeing Paul again. She wasn't in love with him as she was with Ethan, but that didn't mean she didn't care about him enough to not want to hurt him. He was, after all, a great guy. He deserved better than he was getting.

But even as she walked out of the car park and towards the office her mind was going back to Ethan. Had he got the note yet? What was he doing now? Was he still with Amy?

She shook her head. She needed to stop obsessing and focus on the job ahead. The sooner she fixed things, the sooner she could get back to him. She wanted every moment she could get before he left her again.

Paul glanced up when she walked into the wide office space. He straightened from the position he'd been in, overlooking a coworker's computer screen. Then with a small smile he met her midway and beckoned her to his office.

'We'll talk in here, Abbey.'

She nodded in agreement as she felt several pairs of eyes focus on her. Many of her colleagues were aware she had been seeing Paul outside office hours. It wasn't exactly a secret. Many of them even probably thought she had got this latest promotion because of her relationship with him. But anyone who knew her knew she had got it on her own merits. Those who didn't frankly didn't matter.

As the door closed behind her she jumped straight onto safe territory.

'I'll have a talk with the caterers straight away, Paul, and then I'll get changed and go see the people at the venue. This will be sorted in no time.'

Paul walked around her and sat down at his large glass desk. He leaned back in his chair and looked up at her. 'There's nothing to sort.'

Abbey frowned in confusion. 'You've already talked to them?'

He shook his head, his blue eyes looking intently at her. 'There *was* nothing to sort. There never was a problem. Everything's right on track for next week.'

Realization rose quickly into her momentarily confused mind. 'You made this up?'

'I needed to get you back here to talk to me and I knew you cared enough about your job that you'd make the trip.'

Son of a—

She'd known Paul could be ruthless in his business dealings. But he'd been so damned patient with *her*. This was the last thing she'd have expected him to do.

'You played me.'

'Would you have come to talk to me if I'd just asked you to?'

She would have owed him that much. It wouldn't have been the right thing to have phoned him to tell him their personal relationship was over.

'Yes, I would have.'

He didn't look as if he believed that. Leaning forward, he placed his elbows on his desk, his eyes on hers. 'You know I've been through some rough relationships before this, Abbey. I wasn't going to be made a fool of this time.'

'I told you I needed time to sort this out. Some space. You agreed to that.'

He nodded. 'Yes, I did, but I changed my mind.'

His words sent a chill up her spine. He'd never spoken to her with such stern determination. She'd hurt him. 'I never meant to hurt you. I need you to know that.'

The smile was wry. 'You're still in love with him.'

The air went still in the office as he waited for her reply.

'Yes. I'm sorry, Paul, but I am.'

Leaning back again, he quirked an eyebrow.

She moved a step towards him, aware that the ceiling-length windows behind her were giving the office inhabitants a clear view of them. 'If I'd have known he would ever come back I'd never even have thought about a relationship with someone else.'

'I'd like to hope not.'

'There's nothing I can say to make you believe me. But you have to know that the way we were together wasn't exactly a whirlwind romance.' She searched for a way to justify herself.

He surprised her by smiling at her. 'No, it wasn't. I think I've known for a while that it was make-or-break time with us. That's why I proposed.'

It was? His words caught her off guard. It hadn't occurred to her that he might have been having doubts about it himself. But knowing what she did of him, it made sense that he'd have tried something to see what was there. 'You figured if we got married it would mean there was something.'

'Pretty much. And if you said no then I'd know it was time to move on. For both of us.'

'You could have just talked it through with me.'

'We didn't do that kind of thing, you and I. We both had our share of baggage.'

She was stunned by the revelation. All the time that she'd been holding back from him, he'd been doing exactly the same thing. She was no more the one for him than he was for her.

Paul's smile grew at her expression. 'It's all right, I'm fine with this, really I am. You don't need to treat me like I'm some heartbroken idiot.'

She continued to blink at him.

'I think when I came back without you and realized I wasn't heartbroken it made me look at the reality of things. That's why I needed to talk to you. Face to face.'

Abbey felt respect for his honesty. That *great guy* thing again. At least one of them had had the courage to do the right thing. They could have ended up wasting years of each other's lives on something that held no depth or substance. And that would have been a far greater sin.

'I'd have come without you lying about Westside.'

'That remains to be seen. I know you love your job.'

Which raised another question. 'I still have a job?'

His eyebrows raised. 'I may not be too good at picking the right woman, but I know a great employee when I see one.' Then another thought crossed his face. 'You're not going running off to the States?'

She smiled slightly, a flush appearing on her cheeks. 'I haven't been asked to go.'

'He flew halfway round the world to get you. I'd say he'll ask.'

'It's more complicated than that.' She kept her smile on. 'Nothing's ever simple in this life.'

Paul nodded in agreement at her. 'I may not have shown it much, but I believe in romance, Abbey. Something brought him back after all this time. And if you love him enough, then there's still hope there. Look, you have plenty of time before the Westside do. Take some more time off, take as much as you need.'

Abbey felt her eyes well at his words. Blinking them back, she cleared her throat and looked away from his face. 'Thank you.' She looked back at him before she turned to leave. 'I take it back, by the way. You're not a great guy. I think you're a pretty amazing guy. When the right woman comes along she'll be lucky to get you.'

Paul's face warmed at her words, then he grinned and waved a hand at her. 'Hell, I know. Now get out of my office; I have work to do.'

She met Karyn outside the office.

'You're off to the venue already? What about the caterers?'

Abbey grinned. 'There wasn't a problem. Paul made it up to get me back here.'

'He did?' Karyn glanced towards the glass doors with a look of admiration. 'Wow. That's actually pretty ingenious for Paul, isn't it?'

Abbey laughed. 'He's nowhere near as bad as you think he is. Anyhow, it's all sorted now.

We're officially over and I'm actually still employed.'

Karyn's eyes travelled back to Abbey's face and she smiled immediately. 'You're going back to Ethan, aren't you?'

'Yes, I am. As fast as I can get there. I only have three days before he leaves.'

Karyn's hand reached forward to squeeze her arm. 'Tell him, honey. Tell him how you feel. Don't have any more regrets. It's your last chance to have that bloody closure, one way or another.'

She tried the hotel on her mobile again as she cleared the city traffic. It was engaged. How could a hotel in somewhere as tiny as Killyduff constantly be engaged? The employee who was chatting on the phone should be fired.

Setting the phone back in its holder, she concentrated on the road ahead and mulled over Karyn's parting words.

She'd matured a lot since she'd married Ethan. Had life experience she hadn't had when she'd met him. Yet she knew she still loved him. When she'd got married it had been for ever. She'd always believed that was what marriage *should* mean.

And Ethan hadn't changed that much. He had scars now, emotional and physical. The emotional ones she'd probably only touched on, the physical ones she had seen the night before. But he was still Ethan. He was still able to make her smile, warm her heart with a glance, ignite her senses with a single touch. That didn't happen every day. Abbey *knew*.

Their 'one more moment' would never be enough to satisfy her heart. How could it be? Three days of 'moments' were only going to make his leaving even harder. But she knew she couldn't stop the inevitable.

Which begged the question, was she brave enough to try to fight to keep him?

Their night together had been so beautiful. Tender, passionate, *loving*. The Ethan she knew in her heart wasn't so good an actor that he could have pretended all that.

Could he fall in love with her again? He had once. Maybe the dream was possible. Maybe she could hope a little.

The least she could do was try. When the prize could be that good, how could she not?

She smiled wryly at her reflection in the rear-view mirror. Abbey Jackman was going to take a chance and lay it on the line one more time. She had to know.

As she looked back at the road ahead a flash of colour caught her peripheral vision. A blur of red was all she saw before the other car hit hers.

CHAPTER SEVENTEEN

ETHAN mulled over how much his life had changed in such a short space of time. First off he'd learnt he was married. Then he'd travelled halfway around the world to meet his wife. In a few days he'd managed to become fascinated, attracted and then fall for his wife. He'd started to lay to rest the feelings about Jamie; he'd done the right thing and faced up to Amy's feelings for him, allowing her to get on with her life.

It had been a busy time since Abbey's letter had arrived.

He thought about the night they'd spent together. About making love and holding her in his arms until the sun came up. About teasing and laughing over a room-service breakfast. It had just felt so right. As if they'd been together for years. And as he'd looked at her freshly scrubbed, smiling face over the breakfast tray he'd known he wanted to be with her.

Was he hoping too much?

By late afternoon he was missing her bad. By early evening he wondered where she was and took a walk up the street to her house. It was empty. All the cars that had been parked outside on his last two visits were gone.

A sense of foreboding grew. Where was she?

As he walked back to the hotel a frown began on his face. She hadn't mentioned she was going anywhere when she'd left him. But then did he honestly expect that after one night she would report her every move to him?

Hearing music from inside the Fiddler's as he grew near, he poked his head around the door to see if she was there.

'Ethan!' A chorus of greetings met him from inside. 'Come on in and have a jar.'

His eyes glancing around in an unsuccessful search, he moved closer to the bar. 'Hey, Tom. How's that arthritis of yours doing?'

Tom rubbed at his hip. 'Sure it's playing me up all right. I need you to mix me some of that cure of yours again to make it better.'

Ethan grinned. 'Not right now, Tom. Maybe later.' He glanced around again. 'I don't s'pose you've seen Abbey anywhere?'

'Ah, sure, she's away off to Dublin.'

His grin faded. 'You sure about that?'

'Aye.' Tom nodded wisely. 'John, my youngest, works down at the garage at the other end of town and she filled her car there this mornin'. Off back to Dublin, she said.'

'I see.' He frowned hard.

Tom reached out and patted his arm. 'Have a drink, Ethan.'

Much as he suddenly felt the need for one, he shook his head. 'Thanks, Tom, but I have to be going. I'll have to take a rain check on that.'

'What's that, then?'

He managed a small smile. 'It means I hold you to that drink 'til the next time we meet.'

'You'd better. I'll hold you to that.'

'Sure.' He shook the man's hand. 'It was real good to meet you.'

'Sure I'll see you soon.'

He turned and walked out of the bar, his determined steps carrying him back to the hotel as his chest ached. She'd gone back to that other guy. She'd gone running back to him after the night they'd spent together. It hurt like hell. And it made him so angry he wanted to punch something.

Walking through the hotel foyer, he increased his pace. He'd made a damn fool of himself and he hated that she'd done that. He'd actually thought they had a chance, that that whole 'meant to be' thing really could exist.

He was a damned fool.

He took the stairs two at a time and arrived at Amy's door. She answered after his second pounding against the wood.

'Ethan, what's wrong?'

'You change your flight yet?'

She nodded. 'I leave tomorrow afternoon. Why?'

The decision was made there and then. 'Call them back and get another seat. We're both going back home where we belong.'

The Gardai officer took his time taking statements at the accident. Abbey held a square of gauze to her forehead as she answered his questions and focused on his partner as he measured out the distance between the two cars.

It had been so quick. There hadn't even been time for her to brake. And now that she was sitting in the back of an ambulance, all she could think about was Ethan's accident.

It must have been just as quick. Had he been thinking about her when it had happened just as she'd been thinking about him?

She felt the warmth of her tears as they flowed down her face. All it could have taken was a split second. Another accident could have kept them apart as surely as the first one had.

'Take your time, miss.'

She blinked up at the young officer in his dark uniform. He probably thought she was in shock. Maybe he was right. But it was as much the shock of the reality of another accident that had her shaking and chilled. Thankfully, this time everyone was walking away. But it seemed dumb to try and explain this to the officer. How could he understand the glimpse she'd just been given?

'It's all right. There's really not anything else I can say.'

'Well, sure, we have your insurance details and the statement from the other lady.'

Abbey nodded, the movement bringing stars to her eyes. Thank God for her seat belt and the law that had made her wear it. Without it she would have gone through the windscreen instead of banging her head on the steering wheel. She carried a reminder of how hard that strip of material had held her in her seat from the pain across her chest. She hadn't even been driving all that fast.

'I just need to do a breathalyzer test and then you can go to the hospital.'

She grimaced at the humiliation of taking the test. But she knew it was necessary. One thing she didn't think was necessary though: 'I don't need to go to hospital, really. I need to be somewhere.'

The paramedic beside her frowned at her words. 'You'll have to go, miss. You have a quare bump to the head and you'll lose me my job if you don't get looked over.'

She moved her head to the right to look at him and frowned hard when the stars reappeared. 'You don't understand. I have to go. I'll be fine.'

As the officer produced his breathalyzer in front of her she felt a wave of nausea hit her. She wanted Ethan. She had to see Ethan. Everything welled up inside her and before she knew it she was throwing up over the officer's feet. 'Oh, my God, I'm so sorry.'

The paramedic slipped his arm around her shoulders. 'You really do need to go to the hospital now.'

The time in the hospital seemed to go slower by the hour. She'd seen a doctor in the emergency room fairly quickly but the wait for X-rays took for ever.

Her paramedic, Joe as he turned out to be, had asked her if she wanted him to call anyone and her heart had immediately cried out for Ethan.

But fortunately her aching head had the sense to ask for Karyn. She was closer, had a car that could take her home. And Abbey couldn't have done it to Ethan. She couldn't have had some stranger call him to tell him she'd been in an accident. She couldn't have lived with what that would have felt like to him.

As it was, when Karyn arrived, she was pale and pinched with worry. 'God, Abbey, you scared the life out of me.'

Abbey smiled wryly. 'I scared me too. I'm okay though, really I am.'

Karyn looked at her pale face with a look of doubt. 'You don't bloody look all right. What does the doctor say?'

'They took some X-rays. They're waiting to make sure I haven't cracked a rib on the seat belt.'

She nodded as she pulled up a plastic chair beside Abbey's bed. 'What happened?'

'Some old lady pulled out in front of me. She's okay. Shook up too, I think, but they're checking her over. It was just a dumb accident.'

Karyn's eyes widened as Abbey's eyes filled with tears. 'It made me think about Ethan. About his accident.'

Sitting up on the edge of the bed, Karyn circled Abbey's shoulders with one arm and squeezed her tight. 'Of course it did, hon. But you're all right. You're all right and we'll have you out of here in no time.'

'I need to see him.'

'Of course you do. I'll drive you back to Killyduff as soon as we leave.'

Abbey nodded as a sob choked her throat. 'Thank you.'

A doctor appeared from behind the curtain. 'Well, the good news is no fractures or breaks.'

'That's great.' Karyn squeezed her shoulders again.

'But we still need to keep you in overnight because of the bump to the head and the fact you were sick. There's still a chance you may have concussion.'

Abbey's eyes widened. 'I have to go home.' Suddenly it was desperately important she see Ethan to tell him how she felt. It felt as if she was running out of time.

'I'll call him and tell him you'll be there tomorrow. It'll be fine, hon. Don't worry.'

Amy looked at Ethan with suspicion as she packed the remainder of her things in her case.

'Where'd you go last night?' She'd tried his room an hour after he'd come to get her to change the flight. 'I went looking for you.'

He'd felt like a trapped lion in his room. There was no way on God's earth he'd been going to sleep. 'I went to the local pub for a few drinks with some friends.'

'What time did you get back?'

He shrugged. 'I think I stumbled back about three-ish. They have this tradition called a "lock-in".'

'Oh.'

'More like ''Ouch''.'

'Mmm. A hangover, then.' She folded a sweater and placed it in her case. 'Self-inflicted, so I have absolutely no sympathy for you.'

'Thanks, friend.'

'No problem.' She folded another item and then held it against her breasts as she studied him. 'You sure about leaving early?'

'Yep.'

'You want to tell me what happened?'

He glared up at her. 'So you can say I told you so?'

'No.' She sat down beside him. 'So I can understand why you're feeling this bad. You didn't want to go anywhere yesterday afternoon.'

Ethan took a deep breath and looked at her from the corner of his eye. 'She went back to that other guy.'

Amy's eyes widened. 'Really? Did she say goodbye?'

'No.' And that had bugged him the most. After everything they had shared surely it wouldn't have been too much to expect she'd say goodbye to him. But then it wasn't as if he really knew her, was it? So how would he know what to expect? 'You were right. I was obviously chasing after something that wasn't there.'

Amy was silent for a second, then, 'Hurts, doesn't it?'

His answer came out on a whoosh of breath. 'Yes.' Then he managed a small smile for her. 'But I'll get over it in time.'

'You don't want to try and talk to her before you go?'

He shook his head. 'Uh-uh. I think I have more than enough egg on my face.'

'Okay, then.' She nodded and stood to finish her packing. 'Then we better get a move on. It's gonna take us half the day to get a cab from this place. That damned receptionist was on the phone for hours before I could get a line to change your flight.' She glanced at him with a small smile. 'Boyfriend trouble, apparently.'

'Relationships suck, don't they?'

CHAPTER EIGHTEEN

ABBEY had never been so glad to reach the outskirts of Killyduff. Though pretty much every field for miles was the outskirts.

Her heart pounded as they got closer to the main street and the hotel. She pulled down the visor and studied her appearance. Apart from being pale and a huge bruise on her forehead she looked as well as could be expected for someone who was about to put that pounding heart on the line.

'Nervous?' Karyn smiled across at her.

'Me? Nah, I go around telling men they're the love of my life all the time. Hadn't you noticed?'

She laughed. 'Must have missed that part.'

Abbey pushed the visor back into place as they pulled up outside the hotel. 'Wish me luck.'

'You'll be fine, hon.' Karyn reached across for a hug, her eyes glistening as they pulled apart. 'I believe in that fate thing enough for both of us.'

Abbey raised an eyebrow.

'Just 'cos I believe in eye candy doesn't mean I wouldn't eventually settle for some amazing guy.'

Having agreed to meet at the house later—hopefully much later, as Karyn commented—Abbey got out of the car and took a deep breath before walking into the hotel.

She glanced at the receptionist, who was on the phone as she headed towards Ethan's room. That explained a lot.

Her heart was going crazy by the time she reached the hallway. What was she going to say to him? Just look into his eyes and blurt it out? 'By the way, I'm head over heels in love with you…'

Her steps slowed as she got closer. His door was open. She would just have to find the damn words.

She glanced around the door and found someone cleaning the room.

'Where is Ethan?' She frowned as the older woman looked at her. 'Mrs McCoubrey, do you know where the man from this room has gone?'

'You mean your husband?'

Her frown grew. 'Yes, my husband. Where is he?'

'Oh, he checked out this mornin'. Goin' back to America, I hear.'

She ran back downstairs and stood in front of the receptionist. Who was still on the phone.

'Excuse me.'

The girl glanced up at her and kept talking.

Abbey leaned over the desk and pressed down on the phone, cutting off the call. 'I said, excuse me!'

'What do you think you're doing?'

She ignored her protest. 'The man in 204? Ethan Wyatt. What time did he check out?'

'I really don't think—'

'What time!'

'Eleven. Two hours ago. With his girl-friend.' She said the word girlfriend with a small smile. 'Dave Boyd was taking them to Dublin airport for a four o'clock flight.'

She was halfway up the street when Karyn beeped her car horn at her. 'Thank God. How fast can we get to the airport?'

'You sure about this?'

Ethan smiled down at Amy. 'Sure as I can be.'

'It'll all work out the way it's meant to, you know.' She reached up to draw him into a hug. 'For me as well as you.'

'I know.' He squeezed her. 'Come on, then. Let's get these bags out of the way and we'll grab a coffee before the plane leaves.'

Everything was going wrong. They were stuck behind two tractors, there were roadworks everywhere that she didn't remember from their trip up, and as they approached Dublin every traffic light seemed to turn red.

'We're going to miss the plane, aren't we?'

'We're not going to miss the bloody plane.'

Abbey willed Karyn to be right. Why had she left it so long? If she'd just stopped before the car had pulled out yesterday. If she'd just seen Ethan before she'd left. If she'd just told him how she felt before she'd left his room that morning. If, if, if...

She'd decided to tell him how she felt to remove the 'what ifs' from her life. And now she had a million more to add to the list. It just wasn't fair.

'We still have to get to the terminal.' A thought occurred to her already addled mind. 'We don't even know what flight he's on!'

'We know what time it's at. We'll just check the boards for departures and if there's more than one flight to the States at that time we'll split up.' Karyn positively sighed with relief at the sight of the large hangars in the distance. 'We're almost there, hon.'

The departure boards listed only the one flight to America at four, so they both sprinted through the crowds of the large airport. It was three-thirty. Abbey knew they'd probably already have boarded, but her feet propelled her forward. She had to try. She had to try.

But no amount of persuasion would get them through to the departure lounge without a ticket.

And Karyn offered many illegal bribes.

Abbey stretched out a hand to her friend's arm. 'It's okay, Karyn. It's not this poor man's fault.'

'Abbey, they haven't taken off.'

She turned sad eyes to her friend. 'They as good as have. We can't stop a plane for a "what if".'

Karyn's face fell. 'I'm so sorry.'

'It's not your fault.' She smiled as her heart shredded in her chest. 'You can't fight fate, right?'

'You can damn well give it a run for its money!'

The fight had gone out of her. She would maybe manage the courage to write another letter. She still wanted him to know. And that way he could do what he wanted with the information.

But the truth was if he had felt anything he would have stayed. He certainly wouldn't have run out on her the day after they'd made love. The Ethan she loved would never have done that. Maybe she had her closure already.

Déjà vu. As they approached Killyduff for the second time that day she smiled wryly at the thought. Karyn had asked her where she wanted to go after they had watched the plane take off. And she had known straight away she'd wanted to go home. To Killyduff. To her mother.

She needed her mother for the first time in a very long time. Ethan's legacy. It was heartbreaking.

Karyn had tried to keep a conversation flowing on the long drive back, but after a while she had given up. As Abbey had turned her face to the window she had seen the tears in her reflection and known it was time to be quiet. There weren't words.

But as they approached her mother's house she tried again. 'I'll go with you to America if you decide to go and find him.'

Abbey shook her head. 'No, it's done, Karyn. I know that now.'

She'd thought about nothing else the whole way back. She'd taken a chance and had her 'one more moment'. That would have to be enough. It had been his choice to leave. Though the fact that he'd left early would probably haunt her for a long time.

She'd left him the note telling him where she was going and why. He had to have got it. And yet he'd still made the decision to go. Maybe her nemesis Amy had encouraged him. Talked him round as she had before. If she'd been in the other woman's shoes she might even have tried to do the same thing.

Karyn negotiated her way up the street. 'Don't make up your mind straight away well. Have a think about it.'

She would. She'd probably do nothing else for months. But she wouldn't change her mind. She probably wasn't even going to write another letter now. She needed to salvage her pride at least. Ethan was gone.

As they turned through the stone gateposts Abbey looked out her side window at the flowering rhododendron bushes. They had always been her sign that she was home when she was a child. Funny how she'd forgotten that.

'Abbey?'

'I won't change my mind, Karyn.' She sighed a little shakily. 'Ethan would have stayed if this meant anything.'

'Honey...' her voice held a hint of a smile '...he did.'

Abbey looked forwards as the car pulled up in front of the house and there he was. Sitting on the stone doorstep of the large house beside two large bags. *Ethan*.

With her eyes fixed on him she unbuckled her seat belt and opened the car door. Ethan remained still, his eyes following her progress towards him.

She stopped a foot from him, staring at him as if she still didn't believe he was there. 'You're here.'

He smiled softly. 'Yes, I am. Where've you been?'

'Dublin. Twice. Killyduff. Twice.'

'Why'd you go everywhere twice?' His eyes sparkled with amusement. 'You forget something?'

How to hope, possibly? But the spark was beginning to light again somewhere deep inside. 'I went to the airport the second time.'

His eyebrows rose in question. 'Why'd you do that?'

'To stop you from getting on a damn plane.'

Ethan searched her eyes for a sign as to why her words had come out with a tinge of anger. He frowned slightly. 'And why would you have wanted to stop me from getting on a damn plane?'

'Because I had something to tell you.'

There was a long pause as he drank in her words and then he smiled a slow, sensual smile. 'Well, I'm here now.'

'Why *are* you here?'

'As opposed to on a damn plane?' He waited for her nod. 'I had something to tell you too.'

Folding her arms across her chest, she continued to stare down at him. 'Go on, then.' She challenged him with a sideward tilt of her head. 'I'm listening.'

'You first.'

When it came down to it she actually frowned as she said the words. Angry at him for being there and putting her through such agony when she should have been weeping with joy that he *was* there.

'I happen to be in love with you. That's all.'

His mouth quirked at her delivery. 'Oh, is that all?'

It occurred to her that another inch or two forward and she could kick him. 'Your turn.'

'Mmm.' He raised himself onto his feet and walked down the single step it took to stand in front of her. He frowned, distracted momentarily by her forehead. 'What did you do to your head?' He reached out a hand towards it, concern in his eyes.

'Long story.' One that could wait. '*Your* turn.'

'I guess it's not that big a deal either. I love you too.' He shrugged. 'That's all.'

It was so much more than she had ever hoped she would hear him say. At best she'd hoped for a chance to spend more time together, to see if they could make a new beginning for themselves. She'd never even dared hope he might feel something so strong so fast.

'You can't know that in a few days.'

Ethan heard the crack of her voice and knew her anger was subsiding. His voice dropped, low and intimate. 'My mind might not remember all the details, Abbey. But I don't think my heart ever forgot. It just needed a reminder.'

She did what she'd done regularly since he'd arrived and began to silently cry. After today maybe she would stop. 'I thought you'd gone.'

'I nearly did 'til that receptionist remembered to give me your note as I got in the cab.'

That girl *really* had a lot to answer for. 'I'd have been back before you left, but I got held up.'

'Just so long as you got here.'

Staring up into his beautiful face, she finally allowed herself to smile at him. 'I never stopped loving you, you know. And I know you still have to leave—'

He reached out and cupped her elbows with his large hands, bending down until his face was inches from hers. 'Not without you this time.'

Her smile grew. 'We have time now.'

His hold tightened. 'I'm never leaving you again. From now on we don't take any chances, darlin'. You're coming with me and we're going to make a whole new set of memories that nothing can take away from us.'

She managed a nod and a small sob before he kissed her, moving his hands to pull her into his arms.

Eventually he raised his head to whisper in her ear, 'White, no sugar. And scrambled with toast on the side.'

She laughed at him, leaning back until she could see his face. 'What?'

He grinned a wide grin and winked at her. 'I know how you take your coffee and your eggs in the morning now, thanks to room service. The rest I can learn over the next fifty or sixty years.'

Abbey laughed at him, happier than she'd been in eight years. When a person allowed themselves hope, apparently anything was possible.

Ethan kissed her again, making a more leisurely job of it before he grinned down at her again. 'This would be the romantic time to ask you to marry me, wouldn't it?'

'I think we got that covered. Though I could go a second honeymoon.'

He groaned. 'Damn, Mrs Wyatt, so could I.'

EPILOGUE

ABBEY laughed along with Karyn's infectious giggles. 'I still can't believe it, you know.'

'I know, neither can I.' She continued laughing. 'It's hilarious, really. I wish you'd been here for it all.'

'I do too.' There were still dozens of things she missed about home. Some things more than others. But she wouldn't trade the life she had or the years still to come.

'You'll both have to come back for it.'

'We will. I'll speak to Ethan when he finishes playing with his helicopter.'

'Don't you get jealous that he spends so much time with that thing?'

'It's his job, sweetie; he still sleeps with me when he gets back at night.' She smiled when her body still managed to glow at the thought of it. Heaven was definitely waking up with him every morning. 'I'm an amazingly good wife, you know.'

'Well, just so long as the army lets him off long enough to come throw confetti at my wedding.'

Abbey wouldn't have missed it for the world. She'd followed Karyn's romance from a distance for over a year, at first surprised, then warming to the match that made so much sense when she thought about it.

'It will. He's due some leave anyway.' She looked up as her husband came through the door in his uniform. He looked sexy as hell in that uniform. 'And speak of the devil.'

'Ooh, let me speak to him.'

She smiled warmly as a kiss landed on her mouth, the sofa sinking beside her with his weight. She handed him the phone. 'It's Karyn.'

'Hey, how's my best girl?' He reached around Abbey and drew her close to his side. He wasn't home until she was that close. 'You're getting married? When?'

Abbey grinned as he looked down at her and winked. 'I wouldn't miss it. We're due another visit anyway and Abbey went all Irish on me at the sight of green beer on St Patrick's Day. Apparently it's not as big a tradition back in the homeland.'

She nudged him in the ribs.

'And now she's bullying me so I have to see to her.'

There was a comment followed by raucous laughter at the other end of the phone. 'Karyn, I'm shocked. Do you kiss your mom with that mouth?'

There was laughter at both ends before Ethan eventually leaned over Abbey to place the phone back in its holder. He stopped on the way back to draw her mouth into a warm kiss. 'Hi.'

'Hi there.' She smiled lovingly at him. 'How are you today?'

'Better now.' He reached out and began to unbutton her shirt. 'Better again when I do some of the things to you that Karyn just suggested.'

'And you always do everything Karyn tells you to, do you?'

'She has some good suggestions occasionally.' He watched her reaction as his hands touched her warm skin. 'I never get tired of touching you, anyway.'

'I never get tired of being touched.'

As his mouth descended to her neck he mumbled, 'We have an hour, don't we?'

She smiled at his words. 'Is an hour long enough?'

He raised his head to look in her eyes. 'A lifetime isn't long enough. I'm still making up for the missing eight years.'

They'd already shared enough to make up for the space there'd been while they'd been apart. And they still managed to learn something new about each other from time to time. The pain of their separation was long since a dim memory in her mind. There were no regrets. Because they were together and more in love than they'd ever been when they'd first got married. And Abbey was grateful for that every day.

A cry sounded from down the hall and Ethan groaned into her neck. 'Damn.'

'So much for that hour of yours.'

He mumbled into her neck between kisses, 'Maybe he'll go back to sleep.'

'Honey, he's your son. He'll kick and scream like hell 'til he gets his way.'

He raised his head again with a rueful expression. 'You'd think at two he'd be better trained.'

'Give him time, my love. He has radar when you're home is all. He's his daddy's boy.' Her eyes sparkled with love as she reached down to her stomach. 'If you're lucky we'll get a break some time before your daughter arrives.'

Ethan's eyes shone as he looked at his wife. He stole another kiss before speaking to her barely rounded waistline. 'You tell your mom you're another boy.'

'It's a girl. I ordered a girl.' She reached for another kiss as the cries from the hall grew louder. 'Go get your son before he explodes and leaves goo on the walls.'

'Okay, I'm going.' Reluctantly he removed his arm and stood up. Walking towards the hall, he grinned over his shoulder. 'I'm gonna go tell him he's getting an Uncle Paul.'

Abbey grinned. It was a funny thing, that fate game.

MILLS & BOON® PUBLISH EIGHT LARGE PRINT TITLES A MONTH. THESE ARE THE EIGHT TITLES FOR NOVEMBER 2005

BOUGHT: ONE BRIDE
Miranda Lee

HIS WEDDING RING OF REVENGE
Julia James

BLACKMAILED INTO MARRIAGE
Lucy Monroe

THE GREEK'S FORBIDDEN BRIDE
Cathy Williams

PREGNANT: FATHER NEEDED
Barbara McMahon

A NANNY FOR KEEPS
Liz Fielding

THE BRIDAL CHASE
Darcy Maguire

MARRIAGE LOST AND FOUND
Trish Wylie

MILLS & BOON®

Live the emotion